Was she ge[tting] through to [him?]

His twisted smile told her he still doubted her sincerity. But she couldn't tell him her reason!

"Please believe me. I'm on the level, Rik. Really I am." Her voice was a whisper.

"Are you?" he responded softly, with a touch of huskiness. But she still didn't know whether he believed her.

He turned up her face and stared into her eyes—as if he were searching her very soul.

His arms cradled her, his cheek rested on her head, hers against the open neck of his shirt, her ear aware of his drumming heartbeats. Jan closed her eyes, knowing that whatever might happen in the future, she would remember these bittersweet moments to the end of her days.

Lilian Peake lives near the sea in England. Her first job, working for a mystery writer, gave her an excellent insight into how an author functions. She went on to become a journalist and reported on the fashion world for a trade magazine. Later she took on an advice column, which contributed to her understanding of people's lives. Now she draws on her experiences and perceptions, not to mention a fertile imagination, to craft her many fine romances. She and her husband, a college principal, have three children.

Books by Lilian Peake

Don't miss any of our special offers. Write to us at the following address for information on our newest releases.

Harlequin Reader Service
901 Fuhrmann Blvd., P.O. Box 1397, Buffalo, NY 14240
Canadian address: P.O. Box 603,
Fort Erie, Ont. L2A 5X3

LILIAN PEAKE

dance to my tune

Harlequin Books

TORONTO • NEW YORK • LONDON
AMSTERDAM • PARIS • SYDNEY • HAMBURG
STOCKHOLM • ATHENS • TOKYO • MILAN

Harlequin Presents first edition May 1990
ISBN 0-373-11268-8

Original hardcover edition published in 1989
by Mills & Boon Limited

CHAPTER ONE

THE DOOR to the interview room opened and a young woman erupted into the waiting area, the door swinging shut behind her.

'If he offered me the job at double the salary, I wouldn't take it,' she declared, slinging her shoulder-bag into place. 'In fact, I'm not even giving him the chance.' She threw a disgruntled look at the closed door and left, muttering, 'Call that a job?'

Jan stared at the magazine she was pretending to read. Whatever it is, she thought, I'll take it if it's offered to me.

The other two girls conversed quietly, bright expectation having taken the place of the tension that gripped Jan from head to toe. Their interviews were behind them, whereas Jan's was to come. They were still in employment, they had told her so. I just have to get that job, she told herself determinedly.

She had lost hers when the department store at which she had worked as a clerical assistant had been taken over. Anything would do, she'd thought, when she had seen the slightly mysterious advertisement in the newspaper. Anything—almost—would be acceptable as long as the pay was enough to let her go on helping her parents.

'Wanted,' the advertisement had said, 'attractive

young person with strong powers of persuasion.
Rewarding salary. Duration of post: temporary,
i.e. until job requirement is fulfilled. Apply in
writing to Raymond Steel . . .'

'Miss Janetta Hart?' the pleasant-voiced
secretary called from the office door. 'Mr Steele
will see you now.'

He was keen-eyed and very polite, with brown to
greying hair, his figure trimmer, Jan noted, than
many men's of his age, which was, she judged, as
he rose at her entrance, in his middle to late fifties.

A quick, smiling nod sent his secretary into her
own office, discreetly closing the communicating
door behind her.

'Please sit down, Miss Hart,' the man invited,
gesturing to a chair to the right of his desk and
appraising Jan shrewdly as she sank into it.

Jan wondered if he approved of her style of
dress. It was an outfit she had specially bought for
the wearying game of job-hunting, a neat dark blue
suit which enhanced her slenderness, while a frill-
necked blouse added a touch of white. After each
wearing, she'd pressed it, and judging by his
expression her diligence appeared to be paying off.

He seemed to like her fair hair which fell in
softly silken layers to frame her oval face, and the
way her well-shaped mouth curved in an uncertain
smile, while his glance bounced with a touch of
confusion off the bright hope in her intelligent blue
eyes.

His next words were businesslike and precise, as
if he had recited them often.

'I'll tell you my requirements, Miss Hart,'
Raymond Steele said, 'after which I hope you'll
give the position on offer—should I offer it to

you—your careful consideration.'

Jan nodded, and from the few clues he allowed to escape she tried covertly to sum up the man. His round, still handsome face, with its neatly trimmed, greying moustache, bore lines which told of hidden anxieties and problems begging for solutions.

Despite the lush ambience of the room's furnishings, the tall green plants softening the highly charged business atmosphere, there was within the man, Jan sensed, a build-up of stress which, if it did not find relief soon, would surely lead to some kind of personal disaster.

Looking out from his eyes was the same kind of appeal for help that she had seen so often lately in her father's. But her father's arose from the unbelievably powerful voice of his own conscience, taking the blame for the indiscretions of one of his subordinates at his place of employment.

'Dick was working under me,' her father had said at the time. 'I should have discovered what he was up to, should have realised that all that money was disappearing. But I didn't. I was his boss, and as such, I must take the entire responsibility for the company's lost thousands.' Against all the pleas of his wife and daughter, he had resigned. His honour, he had said at the time, would not let him do otherwise. His employers, apparently taking the same view, had not tried to persuade him to change his mind.

Now, Edward and Penelope Hart, in arrears with their mortgage repayments, in addition to being unable to fulfil their many other financial commitments, were in danger of losing their home, their possessions and everything in life they held dear.

Whereas, Jan reflected, this man's mute appeal for help appeared to come from a very private need, his inner world, his emotions.

Her father, she reflected, surprised at the extent to which her sensibilities were reaching out to this perfect stranger, had her mother by his side to share his troubles. Who, she wondered, cared about Raymond Steele's well-being?

All this time he had been studying her curriculum vitae, but his mind did not seem to be entirely on it. Lifting his head, he stared at her intently. Taking a breath, he blurted out, apparently even surprising himself, 'I don't know why you're looking at me like that, Miss Hart, as if——' he paused for the right words '—as if you were X-raying my personality and the prognosis was grim.'

Jan's white teeth caught her lower lip. 'I'm sorry, Mr Steele, but——' I've lost myself the job, she thought, getting to her feet.

'Where are you going, Miss Hart?' Raymond Steele asked, puzzled and seeming strangely hurt. 'You haven't heard the job specification yet.'

She sank back into the chair. So he hadn't dismissed her from the list! He seemed relieved by what he obviously interpreted as her change of mind.

As Raymond Steele outlined the requirements of the post on offer, Jan recalled her parents' hugs and hopeful smiles as she had left home that morning. Even if it involved walking on red-hot coals, for the sake of her parents, she vowed, she'd take the job.

*   *   *

It was not so much the offer of a job that Raymond Steele made as a declaration of discovery. Five minutes through the interview, he operated the intercom. 'I've found the young woman I've been looking for.'

Then he remembered that he had not actually made the offer.

'You're willing to take this challenge on?' he asked Jan anxiously. 'Because it is a challenge. I want my son back, in the business, in my life. He's my natural successor. I want him installed in my place, at the head of Steele Construction, with all the facts and figures at his fingertips. Then I shall feel able to retire into the background, not necessarily to go off into the blue, but there if needed, in an advisory capacity.'

'I'm willing, Mr Steele.' He'll never know just how willing, Jan thought. His smile of relief and thankfulness touched her heart.

He took her to lunch at an expensive restaurant, held her elbow while leading her to the table the maître d'hôtel had produced with a flourish.

Despite her efforts to stop him, he topped up her glass for the third time. 'I lost my wife some years ago,' he told her. He took a ragged breath. 'And somewhere along the line,' he added, staring into his glass, 'I lost my son too.' He took a slow sip. 'Now, as you know, I want him back.'

Jan nodded, full of interest. She was still not quite sure what was expected of her.

'Richard—Rik, his mother always called him,' Raymond went on, 'Richard came into the business after graduating. Showed great promise. I groomed him to step into one of the top jobs.' A deep frown grooved his brow. 'When I offered it to him, he said he wanted out. Not just a vacation, nor even a sabbatical. Out, he insisted, for good. He had a business in mind, one of his own. Boats—he was always mad about boats.'

Jan nodded, her imagination stirred by the courage—not to mention the audacity—of a successful young businessman changing direction so drastically.

'We had a terrible quarrel,' her host went on. '"It's your hobby," I told him, "not your career. What's your wife going to live on?"' He gave a wry, sad smile. 'Wives, my son told me, are a fixture, so they're out. Women, yes, they can come and they can go. But a wife? Never.'

'And,' Jan ventured, 'did he go his own way?'

'Disappeared out of my life. Or as good as. I know where he is, but we hardly ever meet.' His eyes fixed on her face. 'Which is where you come in, Jan. You don't mind if I call you that?'

Jan smiled. 'Please do.'

'And you must call me Raymond.'

'Oh, but I——' Then she nodded, reluctantly. In the circumstances, she had no other choice.

'Since you're going to be mixed up in my family affairs—oh, I know this job I'm offering you is only temporary, until you get results—we might as well dispense with the formalities. Now,' he caught the waiter's eye, 'coffee in the lounge, I think.'

Sharing a sofa, Jan made a determined effort to relax. It had seemed a long day, although it was still early afternoon. She was longing to tell her parents, 'I've got the job,' see their eyes light up with relief, and with gladness for her sake.

Raymond invited her to fill the cups, then stirred his coffee thoughtfully. 'When your mission is accomplished,' he said, 'I shall make you a lump sum payment.'

The amount he stated made her gasp. It would be sufficient to see her through the time it might take to get a more permanent job. Most of all, it would also enable her to help her parents to reduce their mortgage so significantly, their future in the home they loved would be assured.

'I want you, Jan, to persuade my son by——' his eyes flicked up, then down '—by every means you know, to come back to the fold. But beware, my dear, he's no tame sheep. I won't use the expression "wolf" because of its modern connotations, but I must make it clear that your job won't be easy. It might take a couple of hours, it might take days. However long, you'll need to be tireless in the pursuit of your objective. As I said before, it's a real challenge. You do understand that, Jan?'

'I understand,' she answered, holding his gaze, hoping he couldn't read in her eyes her growing apprehension at what he was expecting of her.

'In the meantime,' Raymond added, 'and in addition to the lump sum at the end, for as long as is necessary, I'll pay you a regular salary. In fact, I'll make you an advance payment now.' He felt in an inner pocket, then tutted. 'My cheque-book's at home—I don't always carry it with me. However, I know where I left it. I would like you to come back with me, so that I can hand over the cheque to you at once.'

It seemed to Jan that he was so anxious for her to get on with the job with which he had entrusted her, he wanted no delay in supplying her with the financial means to do it.

His lifestyle appeared to be one of luxury and ease, but Jan found herself growing increasingly certain that happiness did not seem to be a part of it.

As he handed over the cheque, Jan's eyes widened again. Either the man was extremely generous, or his need for his son's return was desperate. This amount alone, she calculated, would be sufficient for her journey and for the few extra items of clothing she would need to buy, not to mention her stay in a hotel while the 'work' he had given her to do was in progress.

As they talked over a tray of tea which the housekeeper had cheerfully carried in, Raymond explained, 'I want Richard back in the business, Jan. I want to hand the reins over to him.' He looked at the backs of his hands spread over the arms of his chair. 'The mid to late fifties, in my opinion, is the best time these days to shed the load. And it's heavy, my word, it's heavy! So I'm middle-aged, but I still feel my life is stretching before me.'

Jan nodded and smiled, hiding her apprehension at this man's expectations and the daunting task she had taken on. Suppose Richard Steele was proof against all persuasion, suppose he refused to do as his father wanted?

'I won't stop living when I give up work,' Raymond declared, leaning back, his palms smoothing his neatly combed greying hair. 'In fact,' he smiled at her warmly, 'I intend to start my life all over again.'

Wandering round the grand living-room of Raymond Steele's house while he answered a phone call, Jan was drawn irresistibly to a photographic portrait of a man who, even before her host informed her of his identity, she knew was his son.

So this was Richard Steele, the man on whom she was being employed to target all the persuasive powers she possessed. His dark hair—slightly unruly, as if that, too, was defying conformity—topped a dauntingly handsome face. The eyes, wide-spread, seemed to challenge the camera, the jaw was stubborn and strong, the mouth wide and unsmiling—holding the faintest hint of cruelty and satire?

He was staring straight at her! Her heart gave a strange, unnerving lurch. Oh, no, she thought, turning quickly from the portrait and looking into the gentler eyes of the father, that was one hunk of a male animal she was not going to fall for.

His looks were stunning, and those eyes of his were saying, 'OK, so try me,' but she'd been hurt once, and that once was enough for her for a long, long time to come.

Paying the taxi driver who had brought her from the railway station, Jan watched the cab go with the curious feeling that it was her last link with the life she had known and might never see again.

Telling herself not to be so stupid, she massaged her neck. It wasn't the journey from London that had tensed her muscles so much as the reception that she guessed was waiting for her once she had located Richard Steele's house.

'Wolf', his father had called him. Now she knew exactly how Red Riding Hood had felt.

To give herself time to collect her thoughts, she had asked the taxi driver to drop her at the end of

the road. It was evening, the sun reluctantly leaving
a cloudless sky. It had taken her longer than she
had anticipated, preparing for the journey.

'It's a tough assignment, I realise that,'
Raymond had admitted just before her departure,
his hand on her shoulder, 'but I wouldn't have
chosen you if I hadn't had complete confidence in
you.'

Jan sighed, wishing not for the first time that the
job she had been offered had been a straight-
forward, conventional position in an office. Which
was, after all, what she had been trained for.

From her bag, she drew out Richard Steele's
picture. Raymond, having seen her studying it, had
insisted that she took it with her.

'At least you'll know my son when you see him,'
he'd remarked.

As she looked at the challenge in those eyes, her
heart beat faster. What colour were they? she
wondered, bringing the picture nearer. Grey like
his father's, or blue like her own? Well, she
thought, tucking the photograph away, I'll know
the answer to that soon enough.

It was a bit like balancing on a wire, she
reflected, taking in her surroundings.

'Whatever you do,' Raymond had pleaded,
'don't tell my son why you're there. Say you've lost
your way, or run out of petrol. Or that you want to
buy a boat and would like his opinion and
someone's referred you to him as an expert—
anything rather than tell him the truth. Because if
you do that, Jan, he'll shut the door in your face or
throw you out if you manage to get your foot over
the threshold. And I mean that literally.'

She sighed, thinking, if I'm going to perform

this circus act and persuade a man to do something without telling him what it is I want him to do, I'd better get started. She took a step, then stopped. If only, she thought, I didn't need that money so much, I'd turn around and . . . But it wasn't in her to refuse to rise to a challenge. Maybe Raymond Steel had been perceptive enough to sense that in the course of their conversation? Whether or not he was on to a winner, she thought wryly, remained to be seen.

Passers-by glanced at her admiringly as she walked slowly along the quiet street. Her fair hair lifted in the breeze, her white cotton trousers emphasising her neat figure, the loose cotton jacket flapping back to reveal the low-cut turquoise sleeveless top and the very feminine shape beneath it.

Expensive residences, many in their own grounds, lurked secretively behind screens of Cypressus and evergreens, holding the inquisitive world at bay. Large cars, even a Rolls-Royce or two, decorated the wide sweeping drives. Between the houses Jan caught glimpses of the river, while sloping lawns and terraced flowerbeds led down to private moorings. And very private lives.

Superior houses, she thought, for superior people of whom, her intuition told her, Richard Steele was sure to be one.

The name and number of his residence was engraved on her memory. And it was there, she realised, a few paces away. Slowing down, she stared at the red-tiled roof, the white-painted walls. It was attractive but not grand, with a 'welcome to all comers' air about it—a house you could be comfortable in, she decided, if you were ever lucky enough to belong there.

Her hand went to her cheek. The wide driveway was packed with cars. Richard Steele was giving a party. What a time to choose! she thought, freezing in her tracks outside the entrance. How could she put her message across? 'Come home, son, your father needs you. All is forgiven, he says . . .'

Nor could she go in there and, in front of all those people, confront the host with a fictitious request for expert advice about boats.

Along the road, a car door slammed. 'Hi,' a male voice called, 'late, like me?' He was young and fair and held a bag that rattled, which meant it was a 'bring your own' affair.

Already Jan was shaking her head, but the young man swept to her side.

'All Rik's friends are my friends,' he announced, 'especially of the curvy blonde variety.' He caught Jan's hand.

She tried to disengage from him, but he tightened his hold. 'Come on in,' he coaxed. 'We need more around like you.'

He was so nice, Jan found it difficult to refuse. 'Thanks,' she managed, 'but I——'

'I'm Tony—Tony Moore,' he supplied cheerfully. 'Who are you?'

'Janetta Hart, Jan for short. But I'm not——'

'Get in there somehow,' Raymond had said, 'even if you have to faint on the doorstep.' What better way than this? she reasoned, allowing Tony to lead her to the front door, which opened with a shoulder-shove on to an entrance half filled with upright bodies, upraised hands holding spilling glasses.

Feminine shrieks filled the air, mixed with male greetings and, 'Look where you're going, Tony—well, who've you got there?'

Tony pushed through, pulling Jan. Groups parted, letting them through.

The room was large, its furniture pushed out of the way. There was a table crowded with bottles and used glasses, side by side with plates of nuts and crisps, half-empty dishes of savouries and filled rolls. From beyond the opened patio doors, Jan saw the sudden sparkle of the river, gold-speckled in the evening sun,

Tony released her arm, hoisted his rattling bag higher and made for the table. 'Don't run away, golden girl,' he called over his shoulder. 'I'll be back!'

Wildly, Jan looked around. In this crowd of strangers she felt entirely alone. Her reason for being there was on her mind. There had to be a better way of doing things than this. Even if she managed to identify the man she was looking for, what was the use of staying here? She would push her way back and out again, locate the hotel she had booked into——*There he was!*

A glass on its way to his lips, he leaned casually against the fireplace, half listening to the attractive woman at his side, half preoccupied with the comings and goings of his guests. Then it happened. His eyes met Jan's and the room spun, back, forwards, round again.

Richard Steele in the solid flesh was even more devastating than the two-dimensionsal photograph in her possession showed him to be. He stared at her, holding her gaze, hypnotising her, turning her heartbeats into a drumroll. Then his eyes narrowed, as if he were sizing her up. What was he thinking? She wished she knew!

With a decisive gesture, he tossed down his drink and rid himself of the glass. Lifting himself upright, he brushed from his arm the possessive hand of the woman beside him. Step by deliberate step he made his way across the room.

CHAPTER TWO

HE WAS there, in front of her, fingers thrust beneath the belt spanning his lean waist, studying her in excruciating detail. This is it, she thought, I'm on my own now. If I fall at the first hurdle, it's outside for me, picked up and thrown out bodily. Wasn't that what Raymond had warned?

'M-Mr Steele?' she hazarded. 'Mr Richard Steele?' As if she didn't know!

It took him a few disconcerting moments to respond. At last, his head inclined. 'Rik to my friends.'

'Oh, but I'm——' Jan cursed her inborn honesty, then smiled to cover her near-error. Who was she to tell him she wasn't his friend? 'I've gatecrashed your party. Sorry about that.' Her eyes held a defiant sparkle as she spoke the daring words. 'You can throw me out if you like.'

He made a faint movement at the challenge, almost as if he were sorely tempted . . . Jan held her breath, had she gone too far? She was here, in the wolf's lair. It had been so much easier to get inside than she'd envisaged. It was her job, truly her job, now she was there, to soothe the wild animal, not enrage him.

'Rik, hi!' Tony returned, placing a glass in Jan's hand. 'Look what I found on your doorstep. Some baby, eh?' He pretended to shove his host away. 'Finders keepers. She's mine. OK?'

His host did not answer, he just kept on looking at the girl at Tony's side. Jan couldn't detach her eyes from his. She tried telling herself to watch out. Stop now. Don't let it happen, not again. Remember Timothy and his refusal to make a commitment, remember his 'live with me or else', and she had chosen 'or else', which hurt like a knife-wound, leaving a scar.

But this man was from another world, man to Timothy's boy, strength to Timothy's weakness. His eyes—there you are, she told herself tensely, they're grey, do you see? Winter grey, cloud grey, with a flash of steel. Oh yes, this man lives up to his name . . .

'Who are you?' His voice was deep, making her tremble inside.

Tony glanced from one to the other, puzzled. 'I thought you two were already acquainted.'

Jan started to reply, found her mouth was dry, her throat like sandpaper. She tried again, running her tongue-tip over parched lips. 'Janetta—Janetta Hart. Jan for short.'

She put out her hand. It was a reflex action, conditioned into her by her formal upbringing. Rik Steel looked at it, failing to respond. Embarrassed, she let it drop.

He seemed, however, to have other ideas. He leaned forward, played his fingers down her arm until they reached her hand. She shivered, just managing to prevent it from showing. He lifted her hand, closed his around it and a shock buzzed up her arm as if his touch had made her come electrically alive.

'Hi, Jan,' Rik said softly. 'Welcome to the party.'

'Hey, not so fast!' Tony cautioned. 'I told you, Rik, this baby's mine. I found her.'

'On *my* doorstep, you said?' Rik's eyebrows arched crushingly.

Tony was plainly not the crushable type. 'If it hadn't been for me, she'd have walked past——'

'No, I wouldn't,' Jan put in, then could have bitten her tongue. Now both men's eyebrows shot upward. She took refuge in sipping her drink. She really would have to be more on her guard.

'You were coming to the party, after all?' Tony asked. He looked around. 'So who's the lucky guy you belong to?'

Rik's hand released Jan's and it felt oddly cold. 'I'm alone,' she pointed out, then checked herself swiftly. She had been about to explain her reason for being there! Well, the time had to come when she would have to break the news, but it certainly wasn't now. 'A—a mutual—er—acquaintance told me I'd have fun if I——' Why did she find it so hard to invent? she groaned inwardly. Well, it just wasn't in her nature to lie, was it?

'Hey, lady,' said Tony, 'you want fun? *I* can give you——'

'Rik?' The beautiful woman with raven-black hair materialised at his side. Her blouse was white and basically plain, but its neckline plunged and with her dramatic colouring, and the chunky gold necklet resting on her pale skin, her looks were fantastic. Enough, Jan thought acidly, to give every other woman in the room an inferiority complex.

The woman's hand found Rik's arm again. 'You're neglecting your *friends*, darling.' She shot Jan a flashing, reducing glance. 'Besides, they want your expert advice.'

Which, Jan pondered, as Rik nodded coolly and left with his lady friend, was surely where I came in? Maybe I should have gone with them and eavesdropped on that advice!

'Some woman,' Tony commented. 'Nadia, she's called, Nadia Beech.'

'It suits her,' said Jan, watching her walk away with a stab of something like envy—for the woman's beauty, she wondered wryly, or for her apparent familiarity with the man at her side? Then she reproached herself. Her visit to Rik Steele's place was strictly for business reasons, which was something she would have to remember, no matter what.

'She's beginning to make it obvious to the world that she's getting that restless feeling about husband number one,' Tony was going on. 'Just look at her following the scent trail of the man she's decided to make husband number two!'

'Oh, but——' Hand over mouth, Jan just stopped herself in time. Rik's father, she'd been about to say, says Rik's sworn he'll never marry . . .

Tony had not noticed and Jan managed to turn her near-blunder into a cough. A friend passing caught his attention. Gently disengaging her arm from Tony's grasp, Jan edged her way through the crush towards the open patio doors.

Outside, she could breathe again, think again, wonder where she went from there. A rowing-boat tugged at its mooring rope where the sloping lawn met the river. Other river craft drifted by, music from their radios floating across the water. Their speed was slow, their occupants preparing to tie up for the night.

As she stood on the patio, music came from behind her too. Someone had put on a tape and, turning out of passing curiosity, Jan saw couples, swaying. The rhythm caught at her reflexes and, while part of her wanted to rejoin the crowd and find a partner, the other said no, stay out here out of harm's way. By 'harm', she told herself, she really meant Rik. Not that he would display the slightest interest in her with his glamorous woman friend clinging to his arm.

'All alone?' One of Tony's friends stepped out from the smoky atmosphere. 'This is a social gathering, love, not a wake!' Before Jan could protest, the man had seized her arm and pulled her inside.

'Jerry, darling!'

He squeezed Jan's hand. 'That's my wife. If I don't go at her call, all hell, etcetera. I love her dearly, you understand? But——' He glanced over his shoulder. 'Hey, her claws are out. I'd better go. Look, don't go out there again. I'll find . . . Rik! My favourite woman's calling. Take over here, will you? Or you'll find one of your lady guests has gone missing again.' He nudged Jan before he slipped away. 'Mine host sent me to get you.'

For a tense moment, Jan thought Rik was going to ignore her. Then he lifted himself upright from the wall, murmured a few words to the beautiful upturned face beside him and made his slow, purposeful way across the room. Reaching Jan, he regarded her, eyebrows raised, hands spread on hips.

He said, on a strangely harsh note, 'Well?'
'Well' to what? she wondered, with a quiver of

discomfort. She coloured, not so much with embarrassment as with anger at his deliberate inaction. 'Don't bother yourself, Mr Steele,' she snapped. 'I like my partner to enjoy dancing as much as I do. Duty dances leave me cold——'

She was in his arms, gasping, holding herself stiffly, resenting the roughness with which he had grabbed her. The music had changed, romantic and sensuous now, and she felt her limbs relaxing, paving the way for an all-over lessening of tension, mind as well as body.

He too seemed to be touched by the melodious sounds, his mood appearing to soften. 'Hi there, Jan?' The words were a whisper, teasing, with a question mixed in.

Eyes bright despite herself, she lifted her head. 'Mm?'

'So tell me, where did you spring from?'

Some time she had to tell him. Why not now? Not yet, she told her better judgement, soon, but—it was heaven where she was. Only a fool would turn around and walk away from paradise. And she was no fool. Was she?

Remember Timothy, the other, saner voice reminded her severely. But this man's not my boyfriend, she answered. Not even my friend. He's just a stranger I've got to deliver a message to, then go on my way.

'I'm sorry I gatecrashed your party, Mr——' His mouth firmed. 'Richard. Er—Rik.' She tried a small laugh. 'Got it! Third time lucky, as they say.'

For some reason, his eyes flickered narrowly, then the lazy look returned. 'Crash any gate of mine,' he countered, charm in his smile, grey eyes flicking pinpoints of gold. 'Break down any door.

My arms would be wide open and waiting on the other side.'

Man-talk, she thought, outright flirtation, sensual overtones in meaningless invitations. She'd heard it before, but from him it sounded different. Dangerous, somehow.

His arms moved, linking around her waist. 'Rest your hands on my shoulders,' he commanded softly. 'Lift your head, Jan. Look into my eyes.'

It was still blatant flirtation, but it was also an invitation she couldn't resist. She was lost in his gaze, floating in its calm seas, *going down, down . . . fighting to come up for air.*

For heaven's sake, she thought, releasing the breath she was instinctively holding, what's happening to me? I'm being paid to give this man a message, change his mind, coax him back to his father. Then, job done, get out of his life, take my cash payment home and use it to give my parents security and peace of mind.

In advance of conscious thought, her hands were shoving at Rik's shoulders, her hips twisting to gain their freedom from his widespread grasp. She had to get away from him and regain the emotional balance she had been seeking outside.

'Something biting you?' he drawled, tightening his hold on her body. The gold had gone from his eyes, giving place to a diamond glitter. 'Hasn't any man lusted after you before?'

Jan winced under the bluntness of his words, her full lower lip pushing out in distaste. 'Whoever said romance was dead was right.'

His eyes changed again, like blue from the sky mixing in. 'You want romance? That's why you gatecrashed my party?'

'I——' Overwhelmingly she wanted to tell him her real reason for being there. 'Rik, I——'

His hand on her head urged it back, his eyes leading the way to her mouth. His lips played with hers, lightly but firmly parting them, then he kissed her in earnest, his free hand cupping her face.

A warmth coursed through her, causing her blood to race, setting her pulses hammering.

'How's that for romance, hm?' he murmured, a curious edge to his voice. 'Soft lights, sweet rhythmic music and——' he held her away and looked her over '—— a girl whose lips say "kiss me".'

'Rik,' she said urgently, 'that's not——'

His eyes narrowed. 'Not enough? You're willing to give some more?' He glanced around. 'It's a little difficult with all these people, but later. Later?'

Why, she wondered, was he looking at her like that? Like an angry man . . . ?

'Rik,' a woman shouted, 'come and join the stampede! We're going for a sail in your cruise liner out there.' She pointed to the rowing-boat lifting and falling in the dusk.

Rik's head shot round and he put Jan from him, following the others, trying to get through to the front.

He had left his warmth behind, and Jan ran her fingertips over lips that throbbed and trembled for more. Hadn't they learnt their lesson? But how could they? Timothy's kisses had never affected her like this.

The evening air was cool to her flushed cheeks as she stood on the patio watching the crowd. Now was her chance to find a corner, staying there until she could make it unobserved back to freedom. It was time she checked into the hotel, anyway.

She hadn't counted on being swept to the water's edge by those left behind in the house. There were shrieks of 'Me first' and 'Look, Tony, there's your doorstep baby. She's escaped Rik's clutches.'

In the act of dropping into the boat, Tony stared round, his fact lighting up. He made a grab. Jan, moving just too late, felt a jerk on the arm pulling her downwards. Crashing into the hard shell forced a cry from her throat.

There was a warning shout from Rik. 'Too many, you idiots!' he yelled. 'It'll sink under your weight!'

Someone else was crowding in on her, female nails clawed at her neck. There were more shrieks, of fear this time as the boat rocked under the excess weight. She was being pushed off-centre and she tried her best to resist for safety's sake, but whoever was pushing her didn't seem satisfied until she was over the side.

The water was cold to her overheated skin, making her gasp with shock. As it closed over her head, she thought, oh, God, no! I should have told them I'm a poor swimmer.

There were shouts and screams. Someone laughed hysterically. A man's voice this time, half joking . . . 'Woman overboard!' As she came up, her lungs filled themselves hungrily with the pure evening air. A man cursed, a woman exclaimed, 'My God, she can't swim!'

Coming up again, Jan realised she was crying. 'I want to live, dear heaven, I don't want to——' She had said the words, not thought them.

'You'll live.' Someone was hauling her up, turning her, swimming with her.

The hard ground had never felt so soft, so sweet, the grass against her cheek so fresh-smelling and cool. Water was being pumped out of her, then, face up, lips were over hers, breathing in, out, in again . . . It's OK, she wanted to say, I'm still breathing. But the lips were surprisingly sweet-tasting, persuasive and—familiar.

Arms she had only just begun to learn about were carrying her, the voice which, even in her exhausted state, had the power to excite her was giving orders, clearing the way, uttering threats if one more fool set foot in the boat.

'Bill,' he shouted, 'get the dancing going again, will you? Nadia, there's more food in the kitchen—you know where.'

'Oh, but, Rik darling, you're dripping wet yourself. I'll help you with——'

'I'll deal with this, thanks,' was the terse reply.

'Hey, where are you going,' Tony called, 'with my doorstep baby? You lay one finger on her, Rik, and I'll——'

The man holding her was climbing the stairs. His shoulder to Jan's white cheek felt solid and secure and next stop to heaven.

He shouldered a door and slammed it shut with his foot, swinging her round and pushing at another door that creaked as it swung. There was the scent of soap, and a woman's perfume hung in the moist air as he stood Jan down and looked her over. Her clothes clung, the dampness revealing every curve and contour.

'Don't look at me like that,' Jan protested, teeth chattering. 'It wasn't my fault. Someone pushed me.'

'Oh? Who?'

She lifted a shoulder. 'Someone.' She knew who it was, but could not tell him 'your girlfiend'. Her hand went instinctively to her neck which was stinging under the stringent effect of the water. He removed her shielding fingers and saw the inflamed scratch marks. Recognition of that 'someone's' identity must have dawned as his lips tightened.

Her body began to shake. 'I'm cold, Rik, so cold . . .' Her eyes closed and she swayed.

He caught her against him, holding her still. Then he half turned her, arm still round her waist, his fingers working fast. Before she knew what he was about, her cotton trousers were hugging her ankles. Her briefs followed and she drew a shaky breath as he lifted her free of them. About to give voice to her indignation, she felt the narrow straps of her top being wrenched down, and for a few electric moments she stood naked before him.

His eyes swept her from head to toe. Then an all-enveloping bathsheet came around her shuddering form, while muscular arms drew her to their owner's hunk of a body.

Her cheek against his whorls of chest hair, Jan pulled in a deep musk-filled breath, finding the smell of him strangely irresistible. She was drowning again, she knew she was, but this time it wasn't the dark, deep waters that were claiming her. It was this man she was drowning in, in his personality, his air of indomitable strength. His hard embrace had the strangest effect, making her want to cling, to press against him, claw at his outer shell and fight her way into the very essence of his being.

To her consternation, the shaking intensified and she knew that it wasn't only the result of her recent frightening experience. It was Rik Steele's closeness, his breath on her face, his hard, irresistible maleness.

'It's OK,' he soothed, stilling her slender, shaking frame, adding gruffly against her hair, 'My God, I really thought you'd had it!'

'R-Rik, I'm so sorry about all this. I——' Was now the time to tell him the reason she had come? She lifted her head and saw how wet he was too, which gave her the answer: Not yet. 'Rik!' she exclaimed. 'Your friend was right—you're soaked through! Don't worry about me. Get yourself dry or you'll catch a——' She gave a sudden, shattering sneeze.

His hands started a swift massage of her body, sliding over the towel in sweeping, unnerving strokes. His touch was gentle yet abrasive, impersonal yet exciting, making her maul her lip in an attempt to control her very feminine reflexes. If he weren't so attractive with his damp shirt opened and loose, his black hair ruffled and still wet from his unexpected dip in the river, his features hardhewn with his concentration on the job in hand . . .

'Any better——?' He looked up and caught her expression.

He broke contact, pocketing his hands. Rocking on his heels, he gave her a down-slanted look full of sensuality and sexual knowledge.

'What is it you're after this time?' he asked. 'Romance again—or just plain lust?'

Jan was furious with herself for being so transparent, and with him for being so quick-witted. The perfume in the air was getting her down—confirmation, if she really needed it, of the

recent occupation of the bathroom by his girlfriend
Nadia. The aftershock of her near-drowning was
coming at her in waves and she sank down on to
the bathroom stool, shaking her head.

'All I want, Mr Steele,' she said, her lips moving against the fluffiness of the bath towel, 'is to
get back into my clothes and out of this
house.'

His hands were gripping her armpits and shaking
her until her head went back. She had no
alternative but to stare up at him, meeting the fire
in his flaring pupils. 'Call me that again, and see
what happens to you!' By the way his eyes were
stroking the glowing skin of her bare shoulders
where the towel had fallen away, she had little
doubt as to what that would be.

Her own glance flickered, then her eyes closed.
Her nervous system was telling her without
warning that, for that day at least, it had had
enough.

Then she was in those arms again being carried
into the bedroom. When the damp towel was
unwound from her too-cool flesh and a cotton
T-shirt was pulled over her head, coming down just
over her thighs, she made no complaint. When she
was lowered to a large bed and a cover pulled over
her, she acquiesced. Eyes large with a faint
incomprehension brought on by delayed shock, she
stared up at the figure that towered over her. With
a slow thoughtful action, Rik towelled his hair,
then dried his bare chest and underarms. As his
hands went to his waistband, Jan realised his
intention and turned her face away.

Intimacy with a lover was one thing, she
thought, although she had never got that far with

Timothy. Nakedness between strangers was quite another. All right, so he'd seen her body. That had been unfortunate but inescapable. But she was darned if any man, whether she liked him or not, was going to force his nudity on her if she didn't want it.

'So it's romance she's after, after all,' he said, watching her action with amusement.

'How clever of you to guess,' she retaliated wearily. 'Lust—in moderation—when added to love is just great. But on its own,' her head came round sharply, aggravating the headache that was beginning to take hold, 'you can keep it.'

'You talk,' he remarked, fingers still at his waistband, 'as if you know it all.'

'You've got the wrong impression,' she returned. 'I don't——'

His trousers hit the ground and, as he hurled them across the room, Jan gasped. But he left his underpants in place and his laughter mocked her misplaced display of indignation.

When he returned from the bathroom, he had donned a change of clothes. Fresh from a lightning shower, shirt-sleeved and tieless, he stared down at her, arms folded. 'What shall I do with you? Push you across and get in beside you?'

With sardonic amusement he watched the bright colour spread over her face.

Angrily she snapped, 'We're back to lust then, are we, Mr Steele——?'

He swooped and fixed his hand around the front of her neck, forcing her head back on the pillow. 'You don't,' he said through his teeth, 'call a man by his surname when you're lying half-naked in his bed.'

She would go down fighting, taking the chance that the shrieks of his guests below would remind him of his role as host.

'Don't threaten me,' she warned, tugging vainly at the hard bones of his wrist. 'You said your *friends* call you Rik. I'm not one of them.'

He drew in his lips, started to speak, but changed his mind, breaking his hold.

'I would like my clothes back, please,' Jan said, doing her best in the curious circumstances to sound dignified. 'I've booked into the Merry Maid's Arms and——'

Brows lowered ominously and Jan realised her mistake. 'Business in the area, have you, then?' he asked silkily.

She cleared her throat for time to think. 'No, I—er—a few days' break, that's all.'

'Pressure of work affecting your health, is it? My word,' sarcastically, 'I've got that rare object, a high-powered female tycoon lying in my bed. Director of a company, are you? Top-flight executive, maybe? What's your line?'

'*No*! No,' less heatedly, 'just—just on leave from my—my job.'

'And what's that?'

Why didn't he let it alone? What could she answer? Tell him the truth here and now, while she was lying in his bed? The whole extraordinary situation hit her forcibly. If she had followed her instinct and laughed, it would have been with near-hysteria. For a few fleeting moments she wished she could wake up and find it had all been a terrible dream.

Despite everything—Rik's desertion of his father, his implacable nature of which she'd caught a glimpse now and then—she liked this man. More than liked him, if she were to be honest with herself. It wasn't her wish to go on deceiving him any longer than necessary. Although, at that moment at least, she decided, it *was* still necessary.

'P-public relations,' she improvised at last. Well, she excused herself, in a sense, that was true. With an emphasis on the 'relations', even if the relationship she was most concerned with—between estranged father and son—was not exactly 'public'.

Sitting up, she swung her legs free of the cover and struggled to her feet. Only then did she realise how weak they were, how the shock of nearly losing her life was still affecting her. She swayed and Rik's arms came round her. His eyes were not idle, skimming her slight figure, appreciating the length of leg and very feminine thigh revealed by the relative shortness of the T-shirt he had loaned her.

She looked towards the bathroom. 'I'll get my——'

'They're too wet. I'll lend you some clothes.' He released her, watching her slump on to the bed.

'I've got a few things with me——' Anxiously, Jan looked up. Another giveaway slip of the tongue.

His eyebrows lifted coolly. 'So it's true you intended having a break?'

'In a way, yes.' She bit her lip, wondering whether now was the time. Not skimpily dressed like this, she decided, half in, half out of his bed. 'They're in a holdall.'

He looked around, puzzled.

'Not here. In—in——' There was no way out.

She had to tell him. 'Behind the pot plant in your hall.' What explanation could she give for her apparently quixotic action in hiding her bag? She held her breath.

His eyebrows shot up again. 'Something to hide?'

Colour flared in her cheeks. 'Of course not!' Her voice had risen in alarm. He really was too darned perceptive. Once again she wished she was not an amateur at the game of deception. 'I—I dropped it—er—accidentally, when Tony pulled me into the house.'

Had he believed her? She couldn't tell.

'There's the phone,' he said.

Jan frowned, looking at the table.

'To tell the Merry Maid's Arms you won't be coming.'

'You mean cancel my booking?'

'Why not? Be my guest. There are plenty of rooms.'

'But I——' She was there on false pretences, and his offer of hospitality made her feel terrible. On the other hand, wasn't this exactly what Raymond Steele would have wanted? She wasn't just in his son's house—she was in his bed! 'Persuade my son by every means you know,' he'd said. He hadn't even added 'within limits'.

But there *were* limits, Jan insisted, and they were rooted deep inside her. That low she would not sink—not even for the sake of her parents' security and peace of mind. Would she?

'Thanks for your offer of accommodation,' she said. 'I'll be glad to accept.'

'I thought you would,' was Rik's enigmatic comment as he moved the telephone within her reach.

He was gone some time and, after cancelling her hotel booking, Jan lay back against the softly padded headboard, wondering if Rik been caught up in the crowd. Had she been right in accepting his hospitality? In the circumstances, she did not see how she could have refused. Raymond would have been delighted with the situation.

'Call me whenever anything significant happens, Jan,' he had directed the last time she had seen him. 'Evenings would be the best time. There's sure to be a telephone in your hotel room.'

The telephone . . . She looked at it again. If she didn't stay in the hotel, she wouldn't have a phone at her disposal. So what better time than now? A few words would convey to Raymond that she'd not only managed to get into his son's residence, but—— She smiled as she leaned across to dial. That was all she would tell him, otherwise heaven knew what he might suggest!

'Hi, doorstep baby.'

Startled out of her wits, she dropped the receiver with a crash.

Tony entered slowly. 'Who did you think I was, then? The boss himself? Is this where he's hidden you away? Couldn't he find another room to put you in?'

He looked down at her as she lay back, still quaking inwardly at the fright he had given her. If it really had been Rik, what explanation would she have given? That she was ringing the hotel, although she had already made the call? He'd have said 'go ahead', then what would she have done?'

'You look pale, Jan.' Tony frowned. 'He hasn't touched you, has he? Because if he has, I'll——'

He curled his fingers, making fists.

'Only to help me.' She smiled wanly. 'It's the unexpected ducking I got. Tony, don't let me spoil the party for you. I'm OK.'

He started to smile back, but his frown returned. 'What are those scratches on your neck? Did *he* put them there? I'll kill him, that's what I'll do!'

Jan stretched out a restraining hand. 'Tony, it happened while I was in the boat. Somebody tried to grab me. Probably trying to stop me falling in.' Probably the opposite, she thought.

'Male?'

Jan shook her head.

'Hm,' he answered. 'No guesses needed. Only one female in this house has nails long enough to do that damage. Where's the bathroom?' Looking around, he made for it, emerging with a tube of healing cream. His nose was wrinkled. 'Nadia's scent chokes me. I don't know how the boss can stand that smell. It'd turn me off, not on.'

Jan laughed, reaching for the tube. Tony held it away, sitting on the bed. 'I'll do it.'

'No, please . . .'

He pushed her back, squeezing a curl of cream on to his fingers. Deciding that, given the time and place, it was wiser to acquiesce than to argue, Jan tolerated his touch on her neck smoothing in the cream.

'Get out of here!' The words exploded into the easy atmosphere.

Tony jumped around and dropped the tube, scratching about on the carpet to pick it up. A hand swooped down and snatched it from him.

'OK, pal,' grated Rik, 'you've done your Good Samaritan act. I'll take over.'

Ruffled, Tony shrugged, pushed his hands into his pockets, mumbled, 'See you around, golden girl,' and ambled to the door. 'If this miserable guy so much as touches you, you know I'm only the next floor down.'

Face stony, Rik watched him go, then turned to Jan. 'My apologies for breaking up a romantic interlude,' he rasped, 'but no woman entertains a potential lover in my bed. Unless it's me.'

She stared back at him, pale-faced, keeping to herself her annoyance at his deliberate misinterpretation of the situation. No matter what, until her job was done she would have to keep on the right side of this man.

CHAPTER THREE

RIK tipped her chin. Part of her wanted to jerk away at once—the feel of this man was far too potent for her peace of mind. The other part of her wanted . . . so much more that she had to impose an immediate censorship on her wayward thoughts.

'Are those scratches painful?' he asked, his glance lingering on her throat.

'A bit.' It was a half-truth. They were throbbing, but she wasn't going to tell him that.

To her dismay, he produced a squeeze of the cream, and Jan had to hold on tight to her reflexes as his fingertips made soothing contact with her skin. Tony hadn't much as raised a ripple on the surface of her feelings, let alone cause this wave of excitement deep inside her as this man's touch was doing.

Under the covers, her hands balled into fists as she strove to prevent her shuddering senses from revealing themselves to Rik's keen eyes. All the same he seemed to guess, shooting her a knowing, faintly amused glance as his fingertips soothed and stroked the wounds scarring her throat.

His hand halted, a finger resting on the throbbing pulse in her neck. He was testing the state of her emotions and there was nothing she could do to hide from him their agitated state. His eyebrows lifted at the hastened pulse-beat and he smiled again, this time with mockery mixed in with a curious touch of cynicism.

'You—you have a magic touch,' she commented, in an effort to explain away her racing heartbeats. 'Like those clever gardeners with green fingers, you must have healing hands. The scratches are feeling better already.'

He put aside the tube of cream. 'My hands have been called a lot of things,' he commented sardonically, 'but never healing.' He indicated the holdall he had brought upstairs.

'I'll——' he began, when there was a crash of glass shattering on a tile floor.

'Holy mackerel,' Tony's voice shouted, 'who's done a demolition job on the boss's crystal collection? Whoever it is is in for it!'

'It's OK,' another man shouted, 'it's Nadia. She's fireproof. Rik's her private property—she can twist him round her little finger. Not just her finger, either . . .'

'Hey, Ken,' Tony called, 'you'd better keep your lewd thoughts to yourself. The lady you're talking about's just said—much more from you and she'll sue!'

There was a burst of laughter, and the party rolled on.

Rik's eyes held Jan's. They were like burning beacons on the hilltops of olden times, she thought, warning of terrible things to come.

Then he was out of the room and down the stairs. Nadia or not, it seemed the culprit was in for deep trouble. Am I glad, Jan thought, sliding back under the covers with a deep sigh, that I'm not the one at the receiving end of Richard Steele's anger!

And I hope I never am . . .

Expelling a deep, sleepy breath, Jan turned on to her side. Her eyes flew open in the darkened room. A deep-down instinct had told her something was not as it should be. The bed didn't feel right, and she was vaguely aware that it was not her own.

Someone, she realised, was in the bed with her, a hard, angled male form that wouldn't give an inch no matter how hard she pushed. Panic rang bells in her head, made her lungs seize up. Rik Steele was lying beside her, arms raised, supporting his head on the pillow!

The covers had shifted and she could see that he was bare to the waist and, who knew, she thought, probably to his toes? A man like this one wouldn't care a darn for the sensibilities of his bedmate, whether he knew her or not, nor whether or not she wanted him there. But she couldn't argue away the fact that it was his bed, after all, and not hers.

From the steadiness of his breathing, Jan judged that he slept. Unless he was acting? In this semi-darkness she couldn't be sure of anything. The moon in the heavens beyond the half-drawn curtains wasn't much help. Then another thought took root and her hands met in a frantic clasp. A palpitating warmth swept through her. *Oh, God, had she or hadn't she?*

Reason took control. A few moments' monitoring followed of her innermost sensations, plus a swift assessment of her physical responses, then her fears were laid to rest. She had never thought she was the kind of person, even in a dream-state, to give her all to a perfect stranger. It seemed, to her relief, that that piece of self-knowledge, at least, had been on target.

Now, if she could slip from the bed without wakening him . . . As she crooked her legs to slide them from the bed, his hand shot out and fixed around her ankle. She half turned to claw at his wrist to dislodge it, but it was as futile an action as it had been earlier when he had grasped her chin.

'Let me go!' she cried, trying to free herself. It was like submerging all over again and becoming entangled in underwater weeds. She was caught fast in his inflexible, unrelenting hold. She wouldn't drown in this man, she wouldn't! 'You've no right to touch me,' she protested fiercely, 'let alone sleep beside me!'

Rik's hands reached out to her shoulder and he turned her to face him. 'First, it's my bed, and I can do what I like in it. Second, if you hadn't gone to sleep by the time I got back, I can assure you I would have hoisted you over my shoulder and deposited you in a spare bed.'

'Why didn't you, then?'

'Because,' his eyes skated over her, the neckline of the oversized T-shirt he had loaned her having drooped low over her white shoulder, 'there wasn't another bed made up. And,' his fingers rubbed softly over her shoulderline, 'because the sight of you lying there, looking so darned *innocent*,' he spoke through his teeth, and Jan wondered hazily why he was angry, 'touched my heart, damn it.' His gaze pinioned her, steely grey like a flashing sword. 'As for going to sleep beside you, what did you want me to do?' He grasped her shoulder. 'Stay awake instead? Because I warn you, when I don't *sleep* beside a woman, I make love to her—like this.'

His mouth descended and his arms drew her all the long, unyielding length of him, and she knew then that he hadn't donned a single garment before getting in beside her. His fingers bumped down her spine, then pushed upward beneath the shirt and round her body to cup the firm fullness of her breasts.

She gasped, attempting to free herself, but it was as useless as using a blade of grass to parry the sword-thrust of his male vigour. Her struggles seemed to excite him all the more, and he rolled her on to her back, shifting his weight until it held her firm and helpless beneath him. She felt the total maleness of him and fought with her own sensations as much as she fought him. As she realised how unequal the struggle was, her body yielded inch by irresistible inch to his domination.

Then his kisses changed, becoming softer and more persuasive, his lips playing with hers and parting them, making free with the moist sweetness of her inner lips. Against her will, her limbs began to co-operate, melting and moving in a kind of helpless delight as his palms stroked, his fingers coaxed.

He was aroused, no doubt about it, his desire for her unmistakable and almost overwhelming. Crunch time was coming, Jan tried to warn herself. Any moment now, and she could be on his list of women seduced and conquered, then abandoned . . .

'No, Rik, no!' she gasped. 'I——' He let her go. Just like that, releasing her, leaving her throbbing, her body screaming for more, her lips bruised and pulsing from the remembered pressure of his.

Backs of her hands against her flaming cheeks,

she lay still, getting her breath. Her hands shook, the desire he had kindled refusing to accept the disappointment of non-fulfilment, unwilling to die decently away.

Well, he hadn't persisted and simply taken what he'd wanted. That much she had achieved. He had respected her wishes. Hadn't he? Or had he never intended to go on to the finish, the ultimate possession?

Slowly she forced her eyes to meet his, and found a frown drawing them together. There was a frightening tightness across his mouth, but to her relief the frown faded and he smiled, although he mocked too.

'Wow, Miss Hart,' he drawled, 'you've certainly got what it takes!' His eyes swept her face. 'Blue-eyed blonde.' They dropped to her breasts which had made their escape from under the T-shirt which had ridden up high. 'Shapeliness, sex appeal, a magnetic symmetry that's almost impossible to resist. Mid-twenties?'

Jan nodded, trying unsuccessfully to tug the T-shirt into place.

'Mm.' Rik eyed her thoughtfully. His hand came out, and she clenched her teeth against the renewed and much too potent touch of him. His palm rested just below her breasts. 'Feel that heartbeat,' he commented reflectively. 'A blonde that's vital and vivacious. Not only that, she's got a response curve that's highly dangerous to a man's equilibrium. Not to mention his blood pressure.' She wanted to ask what he meant, but he went on, 'A blonde with feeling. *With heart*. What a find! What a discovery!'

He kissed her again, his mocking mouth making

a trail from her lips, down, down to the cleft between her breasts. Jan found she was holding her breath, closing her eyes and parting her lips in tense anticipation of yet another taste of his lovemaking. She wanted it—never before had she wanted a man so much. Never before, she whispered to herself, had she wanted a man . . .

He gripped her chin and her eyes flew open. His face was a mask, mouth a forbidding line. 'Now, Miss Hart,' he rasped, 'when are you going to stop pretending? *When are you going to stop acting a lie and come clean with me?*'

It took Jan a few moments to comprehend. Then everything became clear. He knew why she was there! She gasped, shaking free and scrambling from the bed, both hands trembling as she pushed her hair from her eyes. For this turn of events she needed clarity of vision as well as clearness of mind.

'How do you know?' she whispered. 'Have you spoken to your father?'

Rik rolled on to his back, his arms supporting his head. His smile held no joy. 'No,' he answered in a 'guess again' voice, appearing to enjoy her predicament. Enjoying his view of her too, long-legged and flushed, standing near the door as if prepared for flight, embarrassed by the shortness of the T-shirt, the way it didn't cover her thighs.

She dived for her suitcase, dragging out some underwear and jeans, pulling them on. His smile broadened as he watched her haste.

'Never dressed in front of a man before?' he jeered.

'No!'

'Now tell the truth.'

She would not demean herself by arguing with him on such a personal subject. Feeling easier about meeting his challenge now she was better clothed, she put her hands on her hips. 'So how did you know?'

'About why you appeared so mysteriously in my life?' He shifted to rest on an elbow, his hips making a mound under the cover which was only just high enough to conceal them. 'I knew from the moment I set eyes on you. One look at you and I knew. The way you hesitated and seemed uncomfortable, as if you shouldn't be there. After that, it was no time at all before my suspicions were confirmed.'

Bewildered, Jan wondered how she had given away the vital clue.

'You called me Richard, Miss Hart,' he clipped, swinging upright and pushing into a dark robe which had been thrown across a chair. 'Every one of them—they've all called me Richard. My father's the one person in the world who calls me that.'

'Every—every one of "them"?' she queried faintly.

He approached her slowly, long, strong legs carrying the formidable height of him. 'Three women before you,' he stated, confronting her, hands in robe pockets, head back, eyelids drooping.

If I were an insect, she thought with a kind of desperate humour, I'd want to crawl away never to emerge into the daylight again.

He tipped her chin, his smile grim. 'But you're the youngest so far. They've all been attractive too.

You are the best looking of them all.' His lips twisted. 'My father obviously thought that the others didn't possess enough——' his eyes followed a trail around her curving outline '—sex appeal to influence me.'

'I was unemployed and needed a job badly,' she explained as calmly as she could. 'He gave me one. This one. Coming here to persuade you to go back home was a *job of work*. Don't you understand? He put an advertisement in a national newspaper. He's giving a weekly wage.'

She did not add, and a very large sum of money as soon as my job as messenger is fulfilled.

'I needed the money badly,' she went on. 'I never thought it—this job—would be easy, but I was so desperate, I took it.' She flashed him a look. 'Your father warned me——' Rik's eyebrows rose, eyes cool '—that you might be—difficult.'

'And that I might throw you out?'

Jan nodded, her legs deciding to back-step and move her nearer to the door.

He considered her narrowly, sardonically. 'It's what I did to the other three. But you——' with a stride he covered the ground between them, capturing her shoulders in a punishing grasp '—were cleverer than they were, weren't you, Miss Hart?'

'Cleverer?' She frowned. 'Luckier, maybe. How was I to know that when I arrived you'd be giving a party? I was swept in with the crowd.'

'Using Tony Moore as a cover.'

'Not true! He pulled me in.'

'OK.' Rik's grey eyes lightened, like the first touch of dawn brightening the river. Was he, she wondered and hoped, relenting just a little?

Believing her at last?

His hands started massaging her bare shoulders, pushing the neck of his shirt farther down her arms. She wished he would stop; the touch of him was beginning to turn her legs to water, making her heartbeats hammer.

'So far, my little go-between,' he remarked, 'you've had it all your way, haven't you? Got yourself past my doormat, didn't you? Saved from drowning, spent a night in my bed and emerged unscathed.'

Have I? she thought. It depends how you interpret the word. My body might be, but my heart—this man I know now I fell in love with the moment I saw his photograph at his father's house, he's got my heart in the palm of his hand. But he mustn't ever know . . .

'When are you going to give me my father's message?'

Arms folded, legs arrogantly apart, Rik surveyed her flushed face.

Her gaze lifted boldly to his. 'When you're in a receptive enough mood to give it your reasoned and unprejudiced consideration.'

He laughed at her cool cheek, the sudden warmth illuminating his face. Jan's heart turned over at the change in him, and she knew she would be prepared to give her all to this man if he so much as crooked his forefinger. Like the little children who followed the Pied Piper, she would trot after him to the ends of the earth.

The trouble was that if she did, or so her common sense told her, she'd be trailing along at the end of a long line of other women. And even if they reached their destination and all the other women had fallen by the wayside, Rik Steele would turn round and tell her, 'If it's permanency you're after, you've got the wrong guy.' Hadn't he told his father, 'Women—they can come and go. Wives are a fixture, so they're *out*.'?

All of which added up to the vital question—*wasn't Rik Steele another Timothy*?

He held up his hand. 'There's no need to tell me what you've come to say on my father's behalf. It's "Come home, Richard, back to the fold." That's the message all the others brought. Am I right?'

'Nearly. It wasn't only "Come back to the fold".'

'There's more?' His eyebrows rose. 'What does he want—a loan to subsidise his extravagant lifestyle?'

'He wants to retire.'

Rik frowned. 'Why?'

'He seems to be feeling the "heavy load", as he called it—said he wanted to enjoy the rest of his life. He said he intends to start his life all over again. So he's paying me as an employee, to do a job. The job of persuading you——'

'To take the hot seat in the boardroom?'

'Yes,' she answered, relieved that the whole story was out now.

Walking to the bedroom window, Rik stared out. At the end of the sloping lawn, the river ran by. On the opposite bank, where cabin cruisers were moored in line, people were going about their morning business. They were pegging out their smalls, swabbing the decks; returning laden with supplies, then waving goodbye to their river mates, casting off with a preoccupied salute.

'This sort of life is close to your heart, isn't it?'

Jan said to the broad back.

'Who told you that?'

'Your father.'

Silently she approached, putting a shy hand on his arm. Rik jumped as if a firework had exploded at his feet, but recovered quickly. He looked down at her hand, then her face. An expression flickered, then faded so fast that Jan had no time to catch its meaning.

He did not seem to object to her touch, nor to her pleading as his father's intermediary. Seizing these crumbs of encouragement, she went on softly to his broad shoulders, 'You wouldn't have to put it behind you, Rik, all this,' indicating the river, the boats moving by. 'You'd be free at weekends. You could probably take odd days off . . .'

He jerked to face her, making her hand drop from his arm. 'I could, could I? You've got it all worked out, haven't you?' Coldly his gaze raked her face.

'If that's the attitude you're taking,' she returned, 'there's nothing more I can say.'

Shoulders drooping, she made for the door. What should she do now? she wondered disconsolately. Return to Raymond Steele, confessing failure? Tell her parents she was sorry, but she couldn't help them after all?

Crouching down, she began to repack her suitcase, stuffing stray items back into it. She would leave, taking her integrity—what was left of it after his mauling—with her.

Straightening, she found Rik was watching her, narrow-eyed. It hit her fully then just what her decision would mean. If she went now, she would be turning her back on that money which, for her parents' sake, she needed so much. Not only that, her imagination conjured up Raymond Steele's desperately disappointed face when she told him that she'd failed him. Besides, if she walked out now she would never see this man again, and that was assuming such importance in her mind, it frightened her.

'Leaving so soon?' mocked Rik, hands in his robe pockets. 'In a tearing hurry, are you, to get back to my father and tell him his stubborn son is saying "no" yet again? Even though his mediator this time has the sweetest smile and is the best-looking female of them all?'

Jan wasn't fooling herself that he had meant those statements as compliments. Expelling a short, troubled sigh, she queried, 'You're saying "no", then? Is that final?'

He looked her up and down, his gaze deliberately lustful, his stare resting on the thrust of her breasts against the fabric of his cotton T-shirt that she was still wearing.

'Stay around a bit longer, Miss Hart,' he taunted. 'Who knows, you might get a different answer. If you play your cards right . . .'

The room next to Rik's, Jan discovered, was the only other bedroom which made any pretence of being furnished. All the rest—there were four in addition to Rik's—had unmade-up beds. Also, either the carpets were missing, or there were no curtains.

Compared with his father's way of living, Jan thought with amusement, Rik Steele's lifestyle was casual in the extreme. If this was his chosen way, no wonder he had given up his nine-to-five businessman's existence!

Her heart sank as she faced squarely her chances of persuading him to return to city living. She had to open her eyes to the fact that they were almost certainly nil. It would be rather like trying to uproot a fully-grown tree from the forest and force it into a flower vase.

Opening doors, Jan discovered bedlinen on wooden slatted shelves, plus a selection of pillows. At least, she thought, smoothing a sheet over the mattress, she had a bed for the night. How long she would stay beyond tomorrow, she didn't know.

The answer, she realised with a shock, did not rest with her. It was entirely in Rik Steele's hands . . .

Pulling a clean blouse and underclothes from her suitcase, Jan discovered a bathroom and changed, puzzled by the silence that lay like a blanket over the house. Where was Rik? Downstairs, she wondered, reading the daily paper after a relaxed breakfast?

Apart from herself, the house appeared to be empty, but the scene that greeted her shook her to the core. Post-party debris littered every room. In the black-and-white tiled entrance hall lay the shattered fragments of Rik's crystal wineglasses. Her ears played back the shriek that Nadia had given as they had crashed to the floor.

It started an ache in Jan's head, her nerves already stretched to jangling point by the restless night she had spent in a stranger's bed—with that stranger lying beside her. Would the memory of his kisses ever leave her, or the way his touch had brought her skin to prickling life?

She wondered if Rik had torn Nadia to pieces for

destroying those glasses. Or had she, as one of the men had asserted, 'twisted him round her little finger'—and more besides, as the guest had laughingly added? Had Nadia, Jan reflected, watching the splintered pieces glinting like diamond chips in the sunlight, got round Rik—literally, offering him kisses in apology, and who knew what else? Despite the fact that she was still married to another man?

Shivering involuntarily as a shaft of jealousy struck her at the mere thought of Rik kissing the woman Nadia, let alone making love to her, Jan forced her thoughts in a more practical direction and went in search of a vacuum cleaner.

It took her much longer to wade single-handedly through the piles of dishes. She had found the top of the dishwasher stacked with them and was about to open it when a notice had caught her eye. 'Rik, get this thing mended. Don't give another party until it is.' The note had been signed by six people, all the names being female.

Her arms were up to the elbows in suds when Rik walked in.

'Doing penance?' he gibed, fists on hips, shirt sleeves rolled. His working denims were dusty and paint-stained, tight across his hips and straining around the muscled columns of his thighs.

'No.' She swung round, arms dripping foam bubbles, eyes bright with defiance. 'I've done nothing wrong. My conscience is clear.'

'Her conscience is clear,' he jeered. 'A rare specimen of womanhood—you should be preserved between the pages of a book.' He wandered close, so close his thighs pushed her back against the sink. 'Squashed flat. Under a man.' He caught her shoulders and pressed her upper half to him. 'This man.'

Jan fought against the feelings the pressure of his body was arousing. 'Oh, no,' she said through lips tight with the restraint she was imposing on herself, 'that's a card I don't play. Ever.'

'Want to bet?' whispered Rik, his lips too near for comfort. They touched hers, leaving them quivering for more. 'Not even when you're with my father?'

His taunts angered her so much, she twisted to free herself, but with consummate ease he stilled her efforts and took her in his arms, kissing her so thoroughly that her own arms lifted round him. Against her will they clung, her mouth a willing victim to the onslaught of his.

Then he lifted his head, watching her expression, a faint smile telling her he knew exactly how he made her feel.

'Your——' she had to clear her hoarse throat '—your shirt's wet now, from my arms.'

With a short laugh he let her go, but there was a glint of triumph in his eyes, the kind of look a man has, she thought with dismay, when he knows he's reached way beyond first base and it's only a matter of time before he achieves his ultimate aim.

'I was sent here by your father,' she declared, turning back to do the dishes, then she paused. 'I'll rephrase that. I've been *employed* by your father to persuade you to change your mind where he's concerned. Not,' she fired at him, 'to act as your bedmate.' Now she felt better, she told herself, having put this man in his place, and at the same time letting him know she was not the easy game he seemed to think she was.

His hands swung her round so roughly, she gasped. A muscle worked in his cheek.

'If I'd intended making you my *bedmate*,' he rasped, 'I'd have had no hesitation in the night in taking you body and soul. You were pliant and soft and warm, and your eyes in the moonlight sent little sexy messages.' His hand ran down her back and up over her hips. 'You were inviting and——' his jaw ridged '—no doubt about it, *you were willing*.' He pushed her from him.

Turning back to her work, Jan had to acknowledge that he was maddeningly right—although her common sense had said 'no', her body had certainly been willing.

There was a movement beside her and she saw with astonishment that Rik was drying the dishes. 'There's no need,' she began, but he cut in,

'In your own words, by father employed you to come here and persuade me to return to the big bad world of commerce and industry, not to act as my domestic help. Nor,' his lips thinned, his jaw ridged, 'my surrogate wife.'

'Will you listen to me?' she cried, making her headache worse. 'The only reason I took this job was because I needed one so badly. And the lump sum will——'

'What lump sum?' Rik's voice had an edge like the steel of his surname.

Jan cursed herself for letting that bit of information slip out. She knew now that she had no option but to tell him. This is it, she thought. The handsome face I'm gazing into is already filling with scorn, which means that I'm as good as out of that front door.

'When—if—I succeed in persuading you,' she

confessed, tensing for the final curtain on their
too-short acquaintance, from her point of view
anyway, 'your father has promised to pay me a
certain sum of money——' she named the amount,
and watched his face grow colder '——money I
intend to use——' She stopped abruptly. Her
parents, pride already ground into the dust, had
sworn her to secrecy over their financial troubles.

When he broke in, she breathed again. 'And if
you don't succeed?'

'End of job and——'

'No lump sum,' he finished. She nodded. Rik
looked her over. 'You want that money?'

She nodded, opening her mouth to say 'Yes,
very much,' but stopped herself just in time.

Rik's lip curled. 'So you'll just have to work
harder, won't you, on the object of your mission?'
He moved towards her, hands still in pockets,
eyes slanted down, placing his body against hers.
She was against the table and couldn't move if
she'd wanted. And to her consternation, she didn't
want . . .

'Be pleasing to him,' he was saying, staring with
a taut smile at each one of her features, lingering
on her mouth, which to her horror began to
tremble as if it were inviting his kiss.

'In w-what way?' she queried, to give her lips
something to do.

'Run his errands, maybe. Look after his
needs—and, my father's money-mad little
messenger, my needs are many and very varied
indeed . . .

He watched with mocking amusement the alarm
that spread across her upturned features.

Shifting very slightly against her, he caused her

to feel the heady masculinity of him. At once her very basic feminine responses leapt to life. A faint flush appeared in her cheeks and Rik ran a finger down them, looking with amusement at his fingertip as if some of her blush had come away with it.

The pressure of him against her increased and her inflamed reflexes made her writhe with the strength of feeling he was arousing. He knows darned well, she told herself, what he's doing.

'Will you stop it?' she got out through clenched teeth. 'I refuse to be *nice* to you. Not in that way, anyway—if that's what you mean. I won't——'

'Oh, but you will, won't you?' he broke in smoothly. 'If only because you want that money so much.'

'No, I won't,' Jan insisted, and watched his eyebrows rise again, whether in disbelief or surprise she couldn't tell. 'That's just not my way.'

From outside there came a yell, and a short man with greying hair appeared at the door. 'Hey, partner, I need help,' the man said, 'with assembling this section.' His look from one to the other took in the scene and a slow smile spread itself across his face. 'How come it's taking you all day to say "good morning" to your woman?' He cleared his throat. 'At least, that's all you said you were going to do.'

'A couple of minutes, Mick, then I'll be with you. OK?'

Mick, still grinning, left them.

'What have you been telling people?' Jan demanded angrily. 'Just because you rescued me from drowning, and let me sleep here last night, it doesn't turn me into your current——'

'Yes?' Rik queried silkily. 'My——?'

'You heard what he said.'

'You're dead right it doesn't. But it puts you under some kind of obligation to me, doesn't it?'

'N-not that,' she hit back. 'Not for a million——'

'Not a million, maybe, but a thousand—or two?'

'Just where on your scale of morals,' she demanded furiously, 'do you place me? If you think I'd really stoop so low as to accept a *bribe*——'.

'Heck, man, are you coming?' Mick shouted impatiently.

Rick shouted back and turned at the door. 'What's that lump sum offer my father made you, if not a bribe?' he taunted.

'Payment for a job—a very difficult, almost *impossible job* well done, that's what!' Jan hurled back.

He sketched a mocking salute and left her.

Shaken to the core, Jan covered her eyes. The job she had taken on, and which she had estimated would take her maybe a day, or two at the most, had begun to resemble in her imagination a test of endurance, a mountain to climb whose summit disappeared into outer space.

At least, she thought with a flash of relief, and even a flicker of hope, I'm still here, on the right side of the door. He hasn't thrown me out . . . yet.

CHAPTER FOUR

MID-AFTERNOON, and already she was missing him. With the sun's warmth on her back, Jan pedalled slowly along the towpath on the opposite bank of the river. She had lunched on rolls, cottage cheese and fruit, all of which she had found in the fridge. Rik Steele, it seemed, ate frugally and with high regard for his health.

He had called her mid-morning. 'I'm at the boatyard. What are you doing?' he had questioned in a lazy-voiced way, as if he were picturing her in a very different setting from the kitchen in which she was standing, remembering perhaps the night they had spent sharing the same bed . . .

'Acting as your "domestic help",' she tossed along the line, quoting his own words back at him. He grunted and she asked, 'Shall I cook you some lunch?'

There was a pause. 'Can you?' he drawled. 'Cook, I mean.'

'Not haute cuisine, but my efforts are edible. I can do a bit more than switch on a kettle.'

He laughed. 'What a find you are—a curvy blonde who's as good in the kitchen as—presumably—in bed?'

'That,' she said firmly, 'is my business,' and he laughed again.

'In answer to your question,' he said, 'I usually have a pub lunch with Mick, my mate.'

Jan guessed he was referring to the man who had shouted for his help, the man who had called her Rik's 'woman'.

Now and then she steered her bike to overtake people walking their dogs. Enjoying the exercise on a rusting bicycle she had found at the back of the garage, she wondered idly where the boatyard was.

Level with Rik's house, she stood down to admire its rear view, its lawns sloping to the water's edge.

Somewhere over there, Jan mused, she had fallen—been pushed?—into the water. And it was there that Rik had dived in and hauled her out. At that exact moment, she reflected, my life began all over again—in Rik Steele's powerful arms.

Moving on, she heard the sound of hammering. Across the water a man worked among some wide-roofed wooden sheds. Steele & Mountford, a board announced, boatbuilders and designers. Repairs undertaken.

Stripped to the waist, tanned and muscular, the man hammered at some wide planks. Propping the bike against her hip, Jan stared watching his rhythmic movement, the very heart of her ignoring the warning signals her common sense was sending out, reaching across with all her mental powers to the man on the opposite bank of the river.

Something made the man straighten and stare across. Spontaneously, Jan's arm lifted, waving to him, but he just went on staring. It was plain he had recognised her, but it wasn't only that. There was something about him, watchful, almost predatory in origin, that made her shiver despite the sun's bright warmth.

This was a man in pursuit of his prey—food for

his 'needs', those appetites he had talked about, basic and demanding. Again she shivered, recognising beyond doubt—although not really knowing why—that she was that 'prey', and that he would pursue her ruthlessly and without mercy until the final, conquering spring. When the teeth of that tiger sank into her, she knew she would be helpless ever to escape his hold.

Swinging on to the bike, she pedalled back towards the town, eager for some inexplicable reason to be out of the reach of those eyes.

Nearing the turning which would take her to Rik's residence, she heard a shout and wobbled perilously, looking over her shoulder at the passer-by who had called her name.

'Hi there, doorstep baby!' Tony Moore was gesticulating wildly, and Jan had no choice but to brake and walk the bike back along the pavement. 'Still in these parts, golden girl?' Tony exclaimed, walking beside her. 'What's Rik done, then—hypnotised you so you can't get away from him?'

You could say that, Jan thought with amusement. 'I——' She cleared her throat, searching for a reasonable explanation. 'He—we—thought it best if I stayed on for a day or two until I got over the shock——' Tony frowned. 'Don't you remember? I nearly drowned.'

'Will I ever forget?' They turned the corner towards Rik's house. 'The boss almost went berserk when he saw where you were!'

Which, Jan thought, is nice for my ego, although it means absolutely nothing. Except he wants to send his father's messenger back in one piece.

'Why do you call him boss, Tony?'

'I work for him, didn't you know? Steele &——'

'Mountford. Yes, I saw. Doing what, Tony? Designer, boatbuilder?'

Tony shook his head. 'Boss does the main design work, and some of the building when he feels like it. There are quite a few men on the payroll. Moore,' he pointed to himself, 'keeps the financial fires burning. Successful company, is Steele & Mountford. Mick Mountford's a hard worker, he's OK. Rik's the tough nut. Travels around the world selling the stuff his company makes. Dancing River's the trade name.'

'I like that, said Jan.

'So do a lot of other people. Demand nearly always exceeds supply. Great firm to be in—hasn't looked back since it started.'

What would Tony and his fellow employees say, Jan wondered, if they knew that she was here to coax their boss away from them? And maybe sell out?

'Come for a drink this evening?' Tony's eyes pleaded and Jan was touched. 'I like you a lot, Jan. We were meant to meet. How else can you explain you and me colliding with each other at Rik Steele's gate?' He saw her shaking her head. 'Good grief, Jan, hasn't any other guy told you how——' he cleared his throat loudly '—how sexy you are? Hey, is there one?'

'A man? Jan lifted her shoulders. 'There was, but it's over.'

'Crazy fool to let you go. His loss, my gain. Seven-thirty, Jan?' His eyes, like his voice, were full of appeal. They were standing in the wide sweep of drive to the house. 'Please?'

Touched, Jan hesitated, but hardened herself. It

might—just—annoy Rik, and the last thing she wanted to do at the moment was put his back up. 'Sorry, Tony. But thanks for asking.'

Tony pushed his head forward and thrust his hands into his pockets. Jan could see they were clenched. He was taking it all too much to heart, and that worried her.

'That's OK,' he said with forced lightness. 'It's a novelty finding a girl who says "no".'

Jan heard the bitterness, and was sorry to have been the one who'd caused it.

Late afternoon, booted footsteps on the concrete path to the rear of the house announced Rik's return. Jan was drying her hair after washing it and he stood at the kitchen door, watching her. She coloured at having been caught in such a personal act in a stranger's house.

'You look,' she remarked, trying to cover her embarrassment, 'as if you're measuring me up again for your next meal.'

'Again?' His brows lifted in question.

'Like you were doing this afternoon when you saw me across the river. Like a—a jungle cat about to tear its prey apart.'

Rik laughed, putting back his head. He regarded her reflectively. 'Mm, you'd make a tasty mouthful. Young and tender as you are. Correction—as you give the impression of being.' His eyes narrowed.

She saw that he still was not convinced of her sincerity and dug deep in her brain, seeking a crushing response to his cynical view of her integrity.

'To be chairman of the board of an international company,' she flung at him, 'you need impeccable judgement, especially of other people's characters. If you haven't sorted my vices from my virtues yet, or sussed out my moral code, then I personally doubt your ability to hold that office.'

'You impudent little——' In two long strides he confronted her, seizing her arms and forcing them behind her, gripping her wrists in a single fist. 'Apologise for that cheeky slur on my character, or I'll——'

'You shouldn't have implied,' her flushed face defied him, 'that I've been putting on an act of sincerity and truthfulness. Anyhow, what I said was true.'

'You know it all backwards, and forwards, too—the component parts that go to make a successful company chairman? Maybe you trained as a business psychologist, hm?'

Jan shook her head, her lips trembling at the relentless approach of his. 'Clerical assistant. My job at a department store closed down on me.'

Her lips were parting now, of their own accord. Rik's eyes were on them as he said, 'Then don't pass judgement on my mental attributes, Miss Hart, especially as you know nothing whatever about them.' His thumb rotated softly on her throat below her ear. 'Nor throw doubt on my ability to sum up a person's character even on such a short acquaintance as ours has been. Understand?'

'Then stop misjudging me,' she whispered.

Seemingly satisfied with what he saw, Rik released her hands. With a sardonic lift of an eyebrow, he made for the stairs. Only when he was out of sight did Jan attempt to rub away the bruised feeling he had inflicted on her wrists.

Later, seated on the terrace, they shared a meal which Jan had cooked. Overwhelmingly conscious of the man beside her on the canopied swing seat, she was aware that more often than not his eyes rested speculatively on her.

Leaning back, she was able to avoid his gaze, and the questions it held. She knew he was still trying to place her where his father was concerned; also that one of those questions was the age-old one. In the past, her head had always provided the answer. But this man was different—he had touched the essence of her as no other man had ever done.

Sighing inwardly, Jan stared at the river, stained with the colours of the sinking sun. Two white swans swimming by stirred the brilliant shades until they resembled an artist's palette. In this calm and beautiful evening, she thought, with a kind of helplessness, and with this man beside her, anything could happen. Couldn't it?

The same small boat from which she had pitched headlong into the river the evening before lay quietly at its mooring.'

'I've never thanked you,' she said, staring ahead, 'for saving my life.'

Rik lifted a shoulder, leaning back also and crossing his long legs. 'It wasn't your fault that you found yourself dragged into the middle of a group of half-drunken idiots.'

They weren't the ones, she wanted to tell him, who made sure I fell in. It was . . . She rubbed at her neck unconsciously and the action caught his attention.

'How are those scratches?' The pads of his fingers found her throat, his touch disarmingly gentle. All the same, Jan had to suppress a shiver. She found to her dismay that even that light contact excited her.

'They're not too bad, thanks. Nature's doing her stuff.' She flashed him a smile and an inscrutable expression passed across his eyes.

He closed the gap between them, casually putting his arm round her shoulders. Her heart sang along with the flashing, darting birds, her body electrified by his closeness. The setting sun's reflection on the water was almost blinding her.

'I can understand,' she said at last, 'how this kind of life appeals to you so much. And why you're so reluctant to leave it.'

He laughed into her bright, upturned eyes. 'As a persuader of a problem son to mend his ways and go back home, you're doing a lousy job, madam. You're undermining your own case, you realise that? Nor is it the right way to get that money my father promised you to coax me back into the fold.'

His tone mocking, he pulled her against him. Her head found his shoulder and for a few precious moments she savoured his closeness, the shower-clean smell of him, the feel of his angled body pressing into the soft curves of hers.

A sigh escaped her. 'What you've said is true, I know. But——' The vision she had of her parents' return to the respectability they longed for and, in their daughter's opinion, were entitled to—hadn't her father worked hard for it all his life?—tantalised her. This was the very thing that had spurred her on, and was the reason behind everything she had done since getting the job.

'But?' he prompted.

'Just that if you refused to leave all this, I wouldn't really blame you, not even if it meant my losing this job. Nor even if I have to forfeit that money——'

'Which you want so much,' he finished for her.

Jan looked up at him sharply. 'Need, not want,' she corrected again. His twisted smile told her he still doubted her sincerity. But she couldn't tell him her reason! 'Please believe me. I'm on the level, Rik, really I am.' It came out as a whisper.

'Are you?' he responded softly, with a touch of huskiness. But she still did not know whether he believed her.

He turned up her face and stared into her eyes. It was as if he were searching into her very soul . . .

The kiss he took was warm and deep, his hand straying to caress her throat, then down, down to cup a breast, stroking and moulding until an urgency grew in her, bringing her arms up to circle his neck, her mouth giving back every one of his kisses. His arms cradled her, his cheek resting on her head, hers against the open neck of his shirt, her ear picking up the drumming of his heartbeats. The seat swung gently beneath them and Jan closed her eyes, knowing that, whatever might happen in the future, she would remember these bitter-sweet moments to the end of her days.

The sound of a car drawing up in the near-distance penetrated her dream. She started to pull away, but instead of releasing her he turned her face and kissed her with a kind of demanding tenderness. Was she getting through to him? she wondered. Was he beginning to believe her at last?

'Darling,' said a husky voice nearby, 'you scolded me enough last night by shouting at me for

breaking those darned crystal goblets. There's no
need to punish me all over again by kissing another
woman in front of me.'

Taking his time, Rik lifted his lips from Jan's,
which left Jan wide open to Nadia's scorching
stare. 'Amuse yourself as much as you like, Rik
darling, when you're away on your foreign travels,
but——' she placed her white, unblemished hand
on Rik's shoulder '—when I'm at the other end of
a telephone line, you know I'll always come at your
call.'

Jan turned a burning face to Rik's. He was
standing now, hands in pockets, completely at
ease. 'Please excuse me,' she said, and got to her
feet, setting the cushioned seat swinging.

'For God's sake, Jan——' Rik reached out, but
Jan twisted away.

'Darling,' exclaimed Nadia again on a note of
deep satisfaction as Jan made for the glass sliding
doors, 'let her go. You know,' her voice took on a
silky tone, 'you really shouldn't play easy to get
with all the wide-eyed young women who cross
your path. I've noticed,' she added, her brittle gaze
on Jan, 'that the women you've loved and left in
your life all have the same pathetic look in their
eyes, darling, except me. . .Because I'm the one
woman you haven't deserted, aren't I?'

Her silky voice faded as Jan ran into the hall.

In her room, Jan gazed out. Two figures came
into view, the woman with her arm around the
man's waist, his hand resting on her shoulder,
tanned and smooth and partly bare beneath the
narrow shoulder strap of the slim-skirted summer
dress.

Jan almost cried out at the familiarity their

closeness implied, the way Nadia talked to Rik so intently, her face gazing up into his. It's an impossible job that I've taken on, Jan told herself—not only in trying to persuade Rik Steele to leave the work he loves, but to tear himself away from the woman he loves too! Except that she'd probably follow him, Jan thought unhappily, to the ends of the earth. *I'm beginning to know that feeling, aren't I?*

They were nearing the river now, but Jan wasn't sure they could even see it, they were so absorbed in each other.

The ring of the telephone made her jump and she wondered what to do. But only for a moment. Rik was surely too far away to hear it, and in any case it might be Tony ringing to ask if she'd changed her mind.

Racing downstairs, Jan flung into the room which Rik used as an office and seized the phone to silence it. If Rik tore himself from his girlfriend's side and came all the way in, only to find it was Tony Moore for her, he would be more than angry, no doubt about it.

'Rik Steele's residence,' she announced, her refusal to make a date with Tony ready on her lips.

There was a pause.

'Am I——' the caller cleared his throat '—am I by any chance speaking to Miss Hart? Janetta Hart?'

Jan frowned. Surely the voice was familiar? It certainly wasn't Tony's.

'This is Jan Hart. Can I——?'

'Is my—my son Rik in the vicinity? Can he hear us?'

'Your——?' Then she knew. 'Is that Raymond?

I should have recognised you! Yes, he's here, Raymond, but he's down by the river.'

'I've been hoping to hear from you,' he said. 'How is it you're there, Jan, and not at the Merry Maid's Arms? You gave me their number, but they said you'd cancelled your booking.'

'I've been meaning to call you, Raymond, but——'

'Will you answer my question, my dear? Why are you there?'

Did he mistrust his son so much he thought he might have——? Well, he nearly had, hadn't he—if she, Jan, hadn't called a halt? But, an insistent voice said, it takes two to make love, and you weren't exactly unwilling, were you? Even though, in the end, nothing happened . . .

'I'm afraid I haven't made any progress, Raymond. I—I fell in the river, I'm a bad swimmer, and Rik saved me. There were plenty of rooms in his house, he said, so why didn't I stay? So I did.'

'Was that,' Raymond persisted, seeming puzzled, 'before you told him the reason for your visit, or after?'

'It was after.'

'Yet, even knowing the reason for your mission, he let you stay?'

'I—I think it's amusing him having me here.' The father almost growled his disapproval. 'Not in that way, Raymond,' Jan hastened to add. 'It's a bit like—well, a cat with a mouse. You know, tantalising me. He said I'd have to work hard to get him to do as you want——'

Raymond Steele seemed to be breathing with difficulty.

'Raymond,' Jan was growing alarmed by her listener's reactions, 'Rik guessed before I told him why I was here. He said there'd been others.'

'True,' he conceded heavily, 'and they got nowhere. But they were tough, Jan. They came from a different world. Compared with them, you're like a defenceless kitten. I refuse to leave you to Richard's tender mercies. My son—I did try to tell you—he's not to be trusted where women are concerned. He's a wolf, and he'll tear you to pieces. Pack your bags, Jan. Come back at once.'

'But, Raymond, you gave me a job to do. Raymond,' she moistened her lips, a vision of her parents' disappointed faces making the tears prick her eyelids, 'I can't give up now. I need the salary you're paying me. Especially the lump sum when I've fulfilled the—the job requirement. I can't tell you why, but——'

'The lump sum I cannot pay you, Jan. I shall need it for the next messenger I send to persuade my son to come home. But I'll increase your salary, if you'll do something for me. Come and stay with me, Jan—as my secretary, here in my house.'

He seemed to be waiting for her response, but how should she answer?

'When you stayed here before you went to seek Richard out, our temperaments blended well, you can't deny that.'

Before leaving for her journey, she had stayed with Raymond for a couple of days, typing a few letters for him.

'Well, Jan?'

Raymond's voice jerked her back to the present. I'm sorry, I can't, I just can't, she wanted to say.

But the words wouldn't come. You'd be out of a job again, her other self said, no money coming in, unable to help your parents.

'I'll—I'll think about it, Raymond,' she temporised at last. 'Maybe I'll stay with you for a week or two, until——'

The telephone was wrenched from her fingers and slammed into place. Jan gasped at the fury of the hand that had intercepted and ended the call, the same hand that was spinning her round, digging cruelly into her flesh.

Never had she seen anyone as angry as the man who now confronted her. He stared down, face white, eyes blazing, mouth a rigid line.

'So it's Raymond, is it?' His eyes shot sharp lights, his lips curling in a fierce contempt. His fingers fastened even more tightly on her shoulder, almost forcing a cry from her tight throat.

'He told me to call him that,' she protested desperately, 'because, he said, in taking on the job, I was going to be mixed up in his family's affairs.'

She found it impossible to guess how long Rik had been standing there, within a hand's touch of her, or how much he had heard.

His father's voice had risen in his efforts to persuade her and, standing so near, Rik had probably heard the entire conversation. And put the worst possible interpretation on it.

Her shoulder ached from his bruising hold; her heart ached too, because, long before nightfall, she would be leaving Rik Steele's house and walking out of Rik Steele's life. Rubbing her hand across her eyes, she wondered idly what he had done with Nadia. Vaguely she recalled the sound of a car's engine firing, followed by a spurt of gravel under speeding tyres. Nadia had probably gone.

Raising empty eyes to his, she said, 'You needn't have sent your friend away. I'll be leaving in a few minutes.'

He regarded her pale face coldly, making no response.

'There's nothing more to be said, is there?' she added, sighing hopelessly.

'You could carry on your "work".'

She frowned, then understood. 'You mean trying to persuade you? What's the use? I know your answer already.'

'You do?'

'It's "no", isn't it? How could it be anything else? If only to lose me my job—a variation on throwing your father's "messenger" out.'

He regarded her, ignoring her sarcasm, his jaw rigid, expression unyielding. 'You could do as I suggested.'

'You mean—do everything I can to please you? Run your errands, housekeep?' She drew an unsteady breath. 'Sleep with you?'

His gaze flickered minutely. 'All that.' The muscles in his jaw worked, then his lip curled. 'My God, you actually seem to be considering it! Despite your maidenly protestations that "it's not your way", and that you wouldn't "stoop so low as to accept a bribe". You must want that money one hell of a lot.'

'I can't tell you how much.'

'I can keep a secret.'

Slowly Jan shook her head. 'All the same, I can't tell you.' If only she could!'

'You mean it's for a purely selfish reason, for you own benefit entirely, and you're too ashamed to say so?'

It was better, she decided, if she were to agree. It would save any more questions, questions she was bound by a solemn promise to her parents never to answer to any outsider, no matter what.

Her head lifted proudly. 'What harm is there in wanting something very badly for one's own benefit?'

Contempt flicked over his mouth, and her pride and integrity wanted to shout, don't look at me like that, then tell Rik the whole story, clearing herself in his eyes at last. But her loyalty to her parents kept her lips sealed.

In the near-distance, a horn blared and the distant tones of a woman ignored wafted through the window, which meant that Nadia hadn't gone. She had merely changed the position of her car and had been waiting impatiently for her lover's return.

The door swung behind him and Jan was left with his sprinting footsteps ringing in her ears. He was running to the woman he loved as if he couldn't reach her fast enough.

CHAPTER FIVE

JAN stood in the silence, trying to come to terms with what Rik was demanding of her.

It was an age-old problem, wasn't it? she reflected. How far should you go in sacrificing your self-esteem and all you believed in to help those you love? All right, she reflected, so I love the man in question, but if I did this thing he's asking of me, there wouldn't be the remotest chance that he'll every grow to love me in return—or even *like* me.

She needed time to think, to work things out—and she couldn't do that here, with the possibility of meeting Rik around every corner.

Evening gilded the trees and the edges of the clouds, misting over even as she watched, resolutely blinking away the tears. There was only one thing to do. She would book in to the Merry Maid's Arms. Yes, they said, answering her phone call, they had a room to spare. What was the use, Jan asked herself as she packed her cases, of longing for the impossible? Better by far to get out now, before she gave herself away by a look or an unguarded action, allowing Rik, observant as he was, to guess how she felt about him.

The inn had an air of welcome. Like its name, Jan thought, gazing out at the colourful sign swinging in the breeze. She wished she felt as happy as that 'merry maid' looked: buxom, apple-cheeked and smiling, arms outstretched to all the passers-by.

The sunset's brilliance flooded in, its natural colours outshining the table-lamp's hard brightness. The old and heavy door possessed a latch but no lock, just a bolt that was too rusty to work. The room itself was low-ceilinged with creaky floorboards, its furniture mock antique and solid. The bed was a hefty wooden affair, wide enough, Jan calculated, for three. Sinking on to it and pushing off her sandals, she sighed, pulling with her bare toes at the long pile of the bedside rug.

So what of her future? she pondered. If she signed off here and now, she would be out of a job again, the help she had envisaged giving her parents once more beyond her reach. In her precipitate flight from Rik's house, all rational thought, except that of escape from his tantalising suggestion, had been wiped from her mind. Now, it hit her—the realisation of all she would lose if she quit now.

Down in the the entrance foyer, the grandfather clock chimed eleven. This was not time, Jan decided, to come to any kind of decision, let alone attempt to discover solutions to all the problems that at the moment were crowding in on her.

For some time she lay staring into the semi-darkness. Not even the softly playing radio above her head helped her relax. Lamps floodlighting the ancient inn added a shadowed glow to the room. Restless, she swung from the bed, returning to the window. The music came softly, romantically, making tears spring, regrets struggle to surface.

The ancient latch lifting, the door flying open

brought her swiftly round. 'No, no,' she cried, 'I'm sorry, but you've got the wrong——'

It wasn't a fellow guest mistakenly entering. It was Rik Steele, eyes blazing like the sun that had slid, not so long before, below the horizon.

Jan's heart pounded, her breath coming in short, faint gasps. Rik's furious eyes swept her, taking in the frothy pink nightdress, the bare length of leg, the smooth shoulders and wide-open, startled eyes.

'So, my father's little go-between,' he rasped, 'we meet again. You ran for your life, did you, when you discovered that the price of success in your mission was too high for you to pay? Not even the knowledge of all that money coming your way could help you tolerate the thought of my arms and my kisses, and my body next to yours in my bed?'

With a few strides, he confronted her. His tall, angled figure was clothed in black—sweater and trousers wrapping around the muscular leanness of his body. In the glow from exterior lights, he looked menacing and almost satanic.

'Shall I give a taste of those arms and those kisses she spurned?' His eyes raked her. 'If ever a woman asked for it, it's you, my *merry maid*.'

He seized her wrists and jerked them against his chest, pulling her with them.

'You really think I dressed like this for *you*?' Jan exclaimed indignantly. 'When I didn't even know you were coming?'

'You expect me to believe that? You, with your calculating little mind, no doubt worked out that I'd follow . . .' Rik held her away and looked her up and down. 'Oh, yes, I'd follow you a long, long way, Janetta Hart, for the golden treasure at the end of the rainbow.'

She was hauled against him and she managed to bite back the cry that sprang involuntarily at his punishing hold. The nearness of his mouth that had kissed hers so thrillingly the night before was almost more than she could bear. But it wasn't the same mouth, was it? It was twisted now, with cynicism and contempt, and when it lowered to draw from her trembling lips a lingering, remorseless kiss she shivered under the ruthless impact, ripples of liquid fire stealing over her flesh.

Rik's hands ran the length of her, burrowing under the filmy nightgown and gripping the bareness of her hips. Then they slid sensually upward, moulding the slimness of her waist and settling at last on the throbbing flesh of her breasts.

Involuntarily, a cry came from her throat and her body started to yield, her lips quivering as his kiss deepened into a searching exploration. When he finally lifted his head, she leaned limply against him, head on his chest, lips moist and swollen from the onslaught of his.

The sound of the music wove its way around them, mixing with the drumming beat beneath her ear, the hammer of her own pulses and the sweet-sad song in her heart. The lips that had kissed her belonged to a man in need, not a man in love— wanting to satisfy the male drive the sight and feel of her had aroused, with not even a hint of sentiment or emotion. And certainly not love!

'How far will you run now, my pretty maid?' Rik mocked cruelly. 'Or will you turn and run the other way—into these?' He released her, his arms opening wide. He glanced at the bed. 'It's ready and waiting. Can't you feel its pull?' He went to encircle her again, but she twisted away—away from the danger of his incredible magnetism, the electricity that sizzled in the air between them.

'Where's the light?' he asked, switching on the table-lamp. 'I want to see the woman I'm making love to. So,' he breathed, jaw firming, 'the answer's still no?'

'I told you,' she answered faintly, 'it's not my way.'

Rik folded his arms, head back, eyes narrowed. 'It will be, Janetta, it will be. Very soon now, you'll come to me,'

Jan bit her lip, fighting against the great strength of his will-power, admitting secretly that, if he so much as touched her again, his statement might—just—come true. But she'd resist, to the bitter end if necessary. She wouldn't give herself away, not to anyone, certainly not to a man to whom she was just another lover, there for a night—or maybe two. *She would not dance to his tune!*

Leaning back against the sill, her breath still shallow, she felt the breeze through the open window flick prickles all over her heated skin. Moistening her lips, she asked, 'How—how did you guess I was here?'

'It took me about two seconds. Either you'd gone to my father's or you'd checked in here. I chose the second idea first, since I know Don Heeley, the proprietor, as a friend. Yes, he said, a Miss Hart was a guest here.'

'He shouldn't have allowed you up to my room without my permission.'

'Agreed. But when I told him you were a close— very close—friend, he understood——'

'*Thought* he understood,' Jan corrected heatedly. 'Now what will he think of me?'

'Don's married, with a spirited wife. He understands how things can be between a couple.'

But they weren't a couple! All the same, better that the landlord should think they were in the circumstances.

'Why did you follow me?' she asked, weariness assailing her without warning. Midnight chimed and she longed for the rest this man was denying her.

'Why did you leave?' he countered.

She made an irresolute gesture. 'The suggestion you made—that I should become your mistress . . .' How could she tell him, I needed to think about it?

'So I was right. The idea drove you away. But after your response to me just now,' Rik's eyes stroked her body, 'I know for certain it would take very little effort on my part to break down your resistance. And don't try to deny it, this thing between us is not all on my side.'

He wrapped his arms around her, pressing her to the length of him, forcing her to feel his arousal, his lips bringing her throat and her shoulders to life, and an insistent throb deep down. He was right, Jan thought hazily, it wouldn't take long for him to make her want him enough to give in to his demands, stay a while in this house, living with him, loving with him, until at last, when he'd had enough of her, he might—just—agree to his father's wishes. Then he'd abandon her . . .

She moaned, knowing she would be the loser, yet feeling her will-power draining away. Her lips were putting kisses over his cheek, her hands linking behind his head—when she caught the scent of his aftershave, the lotion he had applied before going to meet his woman, Nadia Beech.

With a gigantic wrench she freed herself, breathing heavily, eyes blazing. 'Get out,' she cried, 'or I'll call the landlord to eject you!'

Arms folded, legs arrogantly apart, Rik looked at her with scathing eyes. 'Try it,' he dared her, 'and see what I'll do to you after I've explained how I was in the process of bringing my runaway woman to heel.'

'You—you . . .' Jan could not find a word strong enough with which to describe her feelings for him. 'You're—you're still warm from Nadia's bed, I'm sure of it. Did you really expect me to let you jump straight into mine?' Rik's face whitened, the skin around his mouth tautening with anger. 'Now will you go?' She had meant to command him to leave, but her wavering voice let her down.

His smile was not a pleasant thing, full of contempt and mockery. When the door closed behind him, Jan's bravado completely deserted her and she crumpled in a heap on to the bed.

Over breakfast, Jan tried to organise her brain. It was hazy with lack of sleep as she had lain, counting the chimes of the grandfather clock, until dawn broke. Even then the sleep that had overtaken her had done her little good.

Her first duty was, she supposed, to Raymond Steele. She had to harden herself to his disappointment and go straight to his house, confessing her total failure—wayward son had closed ears and eyes to father's call. End of mission, end of job.

Then she would have to face her parents. Her

mother's sorrow would hit her hardest, because it was she who had had so much belief in her daughter's ability to solve all their problems.

A waiter hovered, asking if she needed anything else. As she shook her head and pushed back her chair, she noticed the landlord framed in the doorway, disappearing immediately. Emerging from the dining-room, Jan noted vaguely that he was talking to a man whose back was to her.

She hoped the landlord would stay around. When she had collected her belongings from her room—they were packed and ready—she would seek him out and settle the bill.

The man swung round. 'Janetta!'

Recognition came with a jolt. That stranger was Rik Steele, standing guard over the hotel entrance door, plainly determined that she wouldn't escape him this time. The landlord, Jan surmised, must have been keeping watch, no doubt at Rik's request, warning him when she was on her way.

Looking round wildly, she made for the stairs. Rik was after her at once.

She turned, whispering hoarsely over her shoulder, so that only he would hear, 'Go away! I'm leaving. I've got nothing more to say to you.'

'But I've got plenty to say to you.' He gripped her arm. 'Come with me.'

Embarrassed by the attention they were attracting Jan allowed him to lead her back down the stairs. Then she faced him, cheeks flushed, heart pounding.

'I've given up, I'm opting out. Your father will either have to accept defeat, or send another messenger. One, preferably, who's also prepared to act as a p——'

Rik covered her mouth with his hand, then released her, leading her across the empty lounge and through the door into the rear gardens. They crossed a terrace, descended some stone steps and moved down a paved path. The scents of early flowers assailed Jan's nostrils, trees swayed in the brisk morning breeze.

Rik urged her to a stop beside a lily-covered pond, a central fountain raining delicate arcs of water on to darting goldfish and floating greenery. He turned her to face him and she became overwhelmingly aware of the tough masculinity of his shoulders under the dark jersey-knit shirt, the leanness of his hips, the way his thighs pushed tautly against the fabric of his trousers. Not least was she conscious of the rigid set of his jaw, the deep-freeze coldness of his eyes.

'Tell me,' he said, words clipped, 'how much do you want that money?'

Jan cleared her throat, which had gone strangely dry. 'You know how much.'

'So much you'd do anything to get your hands on it?'

Was he repeating his invitation of the day before, or was it a trick question? 'It depends on what you mean by anything,' she answered cautiously. 'I did tell you that what you—you might have in mind just wasn't my way.'

'No? Not even with a ring on your finger?' He smiled sardonically into her startled eyes. 'Your wedding finger?'

'What—what are you talking about?' she asked, bewildered.

'About you and me. Rik Steele and Janetta Hart.'

'You don't know what you're saying,' she

accused wildly, 'you've got a morning-after hangover from your late-night date.'

'Was I drunk last night?'

'I—I didn't think you were.'

'And I'm stone-cold sober now.' Rik pocketed his hands. 'I'm of sound mind and know exactly what I'm doing and saying.'

'And—and you're asking me to marry you?' she asked in a strangled whisper.

'As a condition of my agreeing to my father's request.'

'But——'

'I'm asking you to become my wife, Janetta. Look on it,' he clipped, 'as a job—that job you need so much.'

'But—but wives are out.'

'They are?' His eyebrows shot up. 'Is that your considered opinion about the place of marriage in society today? Or just about me—a judgement, perhaps, regarding my personal lifestyle?'

'No to the first question, yes to the second. But not my judgement,' she went on breathlessly, still trying to recover from the shock he had given her, 'nor your father's. It's your own. You told him, your father said, that women could come and go, but a wife——'

'Might—just—suit me very nicely, when I do as my father wants. As I will if you accept my proposal.' Rik looked her over, eyes narrowed and evaluating, plainly sensually affected by the scarlet jersey trousers and red and white cotton top, not to mention the shape they outlined so closely. He seemed to have to tug his mind back to the subject under discussion.

'A wife,' he went on, stroking her temple and

cheek, which immediately began to tingle under his touch, 'to act as a hostess at business receptions, attend dinners by my side, accompany me to conferences. Even play some kind of role in the affairs of company. Provided, that is, that the contents of the brain beneath this silky hair,' he lifted a few strands, letting them fall, 'are up to it. And, basing my assessment on our acquaintance so far, I'd take a guess that there's a hell of a lot of undiscovered talent under there.'

The fountain went on making its misty music, bouncing on the lily leaves, its droplets dancing in the golden sunshine. The birds continued to sing and swoop, the insects to buzz, even though the world as Jan knew it was spinning like a top and standing on its head.

'Well,' Rik asked at last, 'is it yes or no?'

She could hardly speak, let alone give a considered view on such an important matter.

'To act as a barrier,' he enlarged, his eyelids flickering as he uttered the words, 'keeping other men's wives at bay.'

'Nadia Beech, for instance,' Jan threw into the one-sided discussion. His expression was unreadable.

'The money you seem to need so badly would be yours.' He watched her closely, monitoring her reaction.

Her world began to behave so crazily, she was forced to close her eyes. The breeze stirred overhead branches, some distant cars went by.

Rik's proposition was a bombshell. It was so startling and so tempting, she decided she had to say something, anything, to bring herself down to earth, to dull the dream that was dazzling her with its promise of heaven just within her reach. And an end to the poverty and unhappiness her parents were enduring.

Rik Steele could be—was, in fact, she knew for certain—all she had ever looked for in a man. Could she afford to let this chance he was offering her slip away? The alternative—never seeing him again—made her go cold, but she had to keep her head, even though a miniature typhoon was creating havoc with her thoughts.

'To keep your public image clean, in other words,' she challenged defiantly, knowing the question would annoy him, but not caring in her desperation to hang on to her common sense and put her dreams back in the Pandora's box where they belonged, 'so that under the cover of marriage to me, you could have an illicit affair or two?'

To her surprise, he did not grow angry, but smiled in an enigmatic way. 'Why not? I wouldn't be the first man to offer a marrige of——' his eyes taunted, his gaze sliding down to her thrusting shape beneath her bright cotton top '—er—convenience.'

Jan wanted to say 'no' over and over, to throw his outrageous suggestion back at him. But something inside her would not let her say the words. If she did, she would be saying 'goodbye' not only to Rik Steele, but to the money she needed so desperately.

Wasn't it ironic? she thought. Here was this man offering her the commitment without the love, yet Timothy, to whom she thought she had given her heart—although she knew now that for him, compared with her feelings for Rik, she had felt nothing but warm affection—had refused the commitment but professed the love.

Marriage without the love she longed for, she reminded herself forcibly. Could she see it through? Look at him watching me, she thought, so detached, so uninvolved emotionally . . . regard it as a job, he'd said, with a substantial financial return.

It hurt her to her depths that Rik thought she could be bought. She wanted to cry, at least pretend you've got some feeling for me . . . because my feelings for you have gone so deep I don't know how I could face life without you . . .

'Well, Janetta,' he said, with that curious, heart-twisting tone he used when he said her name, 'what do you say?' Will you accept my proposal—and my money—and become my wife?'

I've longed all my life to marry for love! The words rang in Jan's head, but didn't make it to her lips.

'What more do you want?' Rik asked harshly, mistaking her silence for hesitation. 'Undying devotion? Do you really expect me to give that to a woman who's considering marrying me solely for what I can give her in the way of worldly goods?'

'How can I trust you to give it to me?' If he hadn't insulted her so grossly, by reminding her that marriage to him would be for material reasons only, with emotion, not to say love, an unknown quantity between them, she would have been able to hold the question at bay. As it was, it burst from her involuntarily, needing somehow to hurt him back. 'The money, I mean.'

It seemed she had succeeded in her aim. With a gesture of contempt, Rik reached into his pocket, drawing out a cheque-book. Then he wrote, handing her the piece a paper. It was for an amount so large that she swayed.

'What's wrong? Don't you think you're worth that much? Don't worry, by the time I've finished with you, you'll be worth every penny.'

Her hand thrust the cheque towards him as if it were soiling her fingers, but he dismissed it.

'Take it. As with all business transactions, I like to bring matters to a speedy conclusion, satisfactory to all sides.'

Jan's hand was shaking at his scornful tone, while her brain tried to take in the amount. She longed to be able to tear up the cheque and throw the pieces to the wind, that way restoring her self-respect and proving to him that the money meant nothing to her personally.

But it was a piece of paper that would enable her parents to hold their heads high again, and this, she decided, was far more important than how the others—yes, even this man—regarded her integrity.

'Well?' He seemed annoyed by her silence.

'This is too much, Rik,' she responded shakily. 'You must cross off one of the noughts. Please.' She held the cheque out.

To her surprise, he took it, but immediately reached forward and pushed in into her pocket.

'There's no need to pretend to a high moral code I know darned well you don't observe. Now will you give me your answer? Will you marry me, Janetta?'

Jan had dreamed of a man like this; she'd dreamed also of a marriage proposal one day woven through with joy and love. Well, one of her dreams was coming true. The other? You could live without almost anything, couldn't you, she told herself fiercely, if you tried hard enough?

Her eyes brimmed as they lifted to his. 'Yes, Rik,' she whispered, 'I'll marry you.'

CHAPTER SIX

SOMETHING about her must have reached out to Rik. He looked down at her, a strange half-smile curving his mouth. His finger pressed her cheek and he stared at the moisture it carried away with it.

'What's this for?'

If only she could tell him, it's partly because my parents' worries will soon be behind them . . .

'Is it the thought of all that cash I've put in your pocket?'

His sarcasm grazed her sensibilities, but she couldn't honestly tell him 'no'. There were much more important reasons, of course, none of which he must ever know.

'Tell me why they're there,' Rik insisted.

How could she say—because you're the one man in the world I want to live with for the rest of my life and the thought of doing so makes me want to cry? With happiness, and with sadness, because it's all been reduced to a business footing. Because I know you'll have affairs outside our marriage—you as good as told me that just now—and I'll have to stand aside and watch. And last, but most important of all, *I know you don't love me and never will.*

'No romance,' he probed, 'is that it?'

Smiling through her tears, Jan nodded. Better by far that he should think that was the cause than that he'd asked her to marry him for all the wrong reasons.

'Of course, I should have remembered.' His arms went round her and she let herself slide into them, hoping he wouldn't feel the mad pounding beneath her breast.

'Never let it be said,' he remarked, his voice deep with mockery, 'that I would ever fail to supply the woman I've proposed to with what she wants most in the world, whether it be romance—or money.'

You're offering me all that money can buy, Jan wanted to cry, except the one thing it can't! Jan struggled against him, wanting to give voice to her indignation at his words, but his hold tightened and his lips took total control, preventing even one word of protest from escaping.

His hands smoothed her back, moving down to stroke her hips, lifting again to cup her breasts. There was an angry kind of seeking in his kiss, the way he handled her body, the way he pressed relentlessly against her.

She moaned, swaying against him, gasping for the breath he seemed determined to deny her. Then he changed, his arms taking her to him, his lips softening, giving as well as demanding. And Jan responded, losing the tensions his angry love-making had imposed, reaching up and with her arms curling round his neck, melting into him.

A smothered exclamation escaped him and his hands moved to hold her face, kissing every part of it. A sudden gust gathered the spray from the fountain, drenching them from head to foot, but they just went on kissing.

At last, lifting his head, Rik smiled into her eyes, seeing the drops on her hair, on her cheeks, while she, laughing up at him, ran a finger round his jaw, connecting the water drops and carrying them upward to his cheek. He kissed the dampness on her nose, then tipped her head and buried his face in her neck.

Drawing a shaky breath, Jan exclaimed, 'We're wet again! We seem fated to get soaked together. Oh, Rik, I——' Quickly, she hid her face against his chest, swallowing back the words that had so nearly made their way from her lips, betraying her. *I love you so* . . . Never would she know the luxury of being able to say those words to him.

Rik laughed, then stilled, staring at her. Reality, creeping in, cooled the spontaneous flare of passion. He looked her wet form over, holding her at a distance, the better to see the slender outline of her body beneath the clinging wetness of her clothes.

Her instinct was to turn away from his searing gaze. Folding her arms across her breasts, she hid them, hardened as they were through his caressing touch. But with a cynical smile he reached out and tugged her arms open, the better to view her curving form.

'*Caveat emptor*, as the lawyers say,' he clipped. ' "Let the buyer beware." You're my fiancée now, I'm entitled to look on the woman I've paid for and inspect what I've bought for flaws.'

'Stop insulting me!' cried Jan, almost bursting with injured pride.

He ignored her outburst. 'And what a hell of a lot she cost me! Not only the down-payment I've made, but the loss of my daily freedom to the bonds of the nine-to-five routine.

'You could have said no!' she exclaimed,

facing up to him and trying to free her wrists from his hold. 'Even now you could have this back.' Tugging her right hand free, she pulled out the cheque he had given her. 'You could say sorry to your father, ditch me and go back to all the things you love.'

'I could.' His eyes narrowed and he released her, taking the cheque again, this time easing away the neck of her top and pushing the paper between her breasts, his hand lingering there momentarily. Her heightened colour, the reined-in anger in her eyes, seemed to amuse him.

'If you——' Jan took a choking breath, 'if you insult me much more, Rik Steele, I'll—I'll tell you what you can do with your money, *and* your proposal of marriage!'

'You will?' Sarcasm slanted his fine mouth. 'You'd walk out on all those beautiful clothes I could give you, all the jewellery, all those exotic holiday places I could take you to? *That small fortune I've just given you?*'

Her hand lifted, making for his cheek, but with a lightning-fast reaction Rik intercepted it and with it jerked her hard against him.

His lips had almost disappeared and, when he lowered his mouth to her, his teeth met their softness, cruelly making indentations until she was forced by his pressure and his hand at the back of her head to take the kiss he was ruthlessly implanting there.

A whimper escaped her, she couldn't prevent it, and it, and its tiny plea seemed to touch a responsive chord in him. The punishment he was inflicting turned to an inflaming tenderness, as if he were intent on caressing away the pain he had forced her to endure.

His arms wrapped around her, across the back of her ribs, pressing her breasts to the unyielding hardness of his chest. He released her at last and, with a dragging sigh, she came up for air.

It was like nearly drowning all over again . . . His eyes mesmerised her and she couldn't tear free from his steel-grey gaze. Her lips throbbed and pouted, their moistness fanned and tantalised by his breath.

'More?' growled Rik. 'My beautiful, irresistible fiancée wants more?' He stared narrow-eyed at her swollen mouth, then laid his own on it again, this time with a stroking softness that belied the cynicism in his voice. As she lay in his arms, Jan knew that at that particular moment there was nowhere else in the whole world that she wanted to be.

'Wow!' he murmured. 'The woman that fate— or should I say my discriminating father?—has thrown in my path this time round's a stunner! I'm going to enjoy my relationship with this little messenger.' His jaw firmed. 'Even if she has cost me a——'

'If you say that once more,' Jan got out, struggling to break free, 'I'll——' Tear up that cheque, she had been going to say. But she couldn't, could she, when it would mean so much to her parents?

The breeze played tricks again, lifting the spray from the stone cherub's urn in the centre of the pond and drenching them with it. Jan gasped, laughing too, her face running with water. Rik, his shirt wet through this time, scooped her damp form into his arms and strode with her through the rear of the hotel.

The landlord, in the doorway of the office behind reception, grinned wickedly. 'I see you've landed your fish, Rik, good and proper.'

'I just reeled her in and she came like a lamb,' Rik remarked, looking down into Jan's furious eyes.

'You've mixed your metaphors,' she accused, snapping her teeth.

'Yes, teacher. Thanks, Don, for your help,' Rik threw over his shoulder as he strode up the stairs. 'Got some mopping up to do. That damned fountain of yours . . . I swear the little b——' he glanced at Jan, and finished '—angel in the centre soaked us deliberately. Twice.'

Don's laughter followed them.

In Jan's room, Rik lowered her to the floor. A discreet knock made him pause. 'Towels,' Don's voice said. 'I reckoned you'd need a fresh supply.'

Shouting his thanks, Rik collected them from a table in the corridor. 'Now,' he growled, advancing on Jan's shivering form, 'here we go again. How you specialise in getting wet! Fully dressed too.'

She reached for the top of the pile, but Rik dumped it on a chair and starting rubbing her down, over her clothes, moving up to her hair and ruffling it madly as he dried it.

'No, no!' she shrieked, fighting him for the towel. 'If you don't let me do it myself, I'll——'

He stopped, hands on the towel piled on her head, easing it back with them. 'You'll what?' His grey eyes had darkened, the high-boned planes of his face moving nearer. 'Don't threaten me, Miss Hart, my strength is greater than yours.'

'Please, Rik,' she pleaded, 'I'm still wet. I'll have to change.'

Hands each side of her head, he placed a slow, sensual kiss on her parted lips, then he let her go.

He pushed his hands into the damp waistband of his trousers, his shirt still clinging wetly to his skin. 'We're dining in style, you and I—a celebration. It's not every day I conclude a business deal and find myself the owner of a brand new, very sexy fiancée——'

'You don't *own* me,' Jan blurted out, backing away from the sky-high wall of maleness that confronted her. 'And there's nothing to celebrate. As you correctly said, it's a *purely business* arrangement we've come to, so you can skip the niceties and little loving touches, especially as there isn't a shred of love between us.' Fingers crossed behind her, she hoped she'd be forgiven for the lie.

'Not a shred,' Rik agreed, eyeing her narrowly.

Before she realised his intention, her cotton top had been tugged over her head, the cheque from underneath it going flying. The palms of his hands proceeded to make the intimate acquaintance of the naked and very feminine curves they found revealed in front of him.

Jan bit her lip to help her withstand the almost unbearable stimulation of his touch. 'D-don't, Rik,' she pleaded, pushing at his shoulders, which were about as responsive to her pressure as the wall of a dam.

She began to shiver, and her legs threatened to give under her. Which would put her right where he wanted her, wouldn't it, right there in his arms . . .

'Agreed about the missing ingredient in our relationship,' he remarked absently, spanning her midriff, fingers outspread. 'Do your really expect a guy to *love* a woman who's marrying him solely for his money? Even if she is so darned attractive she drives him crazy with wanting her.'

Tell him you're not after his money, a small voice pleaded. But what would be the use? Jan argued. He would only ask, Then why *are* you marrying me? To which she couldn't give the true answer, either now, or ever.

'Which means we're b-back to lust,' she riposted through gritted teeth. 'Will you stop *mauling* me?'

Rik looked her over, eyebrows raised, plainly enjoying her heightened colour, her teeth-gritting efforts to prevent herself from responding to the caress of his roaming hands. Then he let her go, watching with deep amusement her haste in pulling her cotton shirt back over her head.

'OK, we'll call it a business deal,' he was saying, a sardonic gleam in his eyes. 'I've made a takeover bid which has been accepted. Winner takes loser for a compensatory meal.'

'To compensate for what?' Jan exlaimed.

'Loss of freedom of movement on the loser's part, loss of her ability to decide her own destiny, submission to the controlling party's whims and fancies.' Now his gaze held a satiric gleam.

'You haven't *bought* me, she insisted, eyes flashing indignantly. 'In fact, you can have the money back that you gave me. Anyway,' she held her head high, 'it wasn't a gift. It was part of the deal I made with your father. It took the place of that lump sum he promised me if I ever managed to deliver his erring son back into his keeping.'

Bending down, she retrieved the cheque from the floor and stuffed it into Rik's trouser pocket. His hand slapped on to hers, trapping it there, and try as she might she couldn't remove it. The intense maleness of his physique brought to flaring life her own pulsating and very feminine responses, the unyielding bone beneath the layer of lean flesh equalling the hardness which, she had begun to learn to her cost, lay just beneath the surface of his character.

'You can take the money back,' she responded heatedly. 'I know your father will keep his promise now you've said you intend to do as he wants. And *he* won't make any outrageous conditions as you've done, about my becoming his puppet and for ever more dancing to his tune——'

'So my father's perfect?' Rik returned sarcastically.

'Of course he's not perfect. No one is in this world. Not even Rik Steele.'

He regarded her, eyes glittering like the sun on a stormy sea. Then, slowly, deliberately, he rubbed the palm of her hand up and down his hip until her colour rose at the feel of his body beneath her touch. His smile was hard as he pulled her closer, half turning her and putting his mouth to hers, taking over and forcing her lips to part for his invasion.

Her own swift and heated response to his domination shook her to the depths. All the same, the last thing she wanted was to break free, no matter what he might think of her. She wanted to lie there timelessly, while his lips and touch wrought havoc with her senses.

Downstairs the grandfather clock chimed and Rik lifted his head. 'You're coming with me, back to my house. Which is where you belong now you're my wife-to-be.' He looked around.

'But, Rik——'

'Your cases are packed,' he said irritably. 'Where the hell did you think you were going?'

'Home. I removed all my things from your house last night.'

His gaze darkened. 'From now on, my home is your home. Remember that.'

'But the room I'm renting——'

'I'll settle that, plus cash in lieu of notice. How much do you owe?' Jan told him. 'Peanuts,' he dismissed. 'You see,' his lip curled, 'what a prize you've got yourself in the way of a husband. Money to burn, all your financial worries behind you. Haven't you done well?'

'It was your idea, not mine,' she blazed at him, 'that I'd have to agree to marry you as a condition of your return to the parental fold.'

'You could have said no,' he riposted, tossing her words back at her. 'You're still free,' he went to the door, 'to turn me down.' A mocking smile flitted over his lips. He had called her bluff and he knew it.

'I—I can't,' she answered flatly. *If only she could!*

'No,' Rik walked back, head slightly lowered, 'you can't resist the magnetic power of this money, can you?' He drew the cheque for his pocket where she had placed it and dropped it on to the bed. 'The thought of your bank account almost at nil, when it could be bursting at the seams with this kind of cash, makes you ready for anything, doesn't it, even giving your not-so-pure self into the legal keeping of a man who's *bought* you with it?'

Jan opened her mouth to protest, but he cut her short, consulting his watch with a businesslike briskness. 'Ten minutes, then I'll be back. Change if you must, but make it snappy.'

Lifting a couple of towels from the pile the landlord had provided, he rubbed at his hair as he left.

It was a little like coming home, after all, Jan thought, staring round at the familiar furnishings of her room in Rik's riverside residence.

She had unpacked and her clothes were back in the wardrobes and drawers as if they had never been away. Rik had gone to his work, telling her to make herself at home, with an emphasis on the last word. Whether it would prove possible to do as he had commanded remained to be seen. Too many questions remained unanswered for her to be able to absorb completely into her system her altered circumstances, not to mention her changed status.

It was her parents who were mainly on her mind, with Raymond Steele, the unwitting cause of the total divergence of her life from its hitherto accepted path, being firmly on her conscience.

When she had suggested to Rik that he might telephone his father and put him out of his misery, Rik had agreed, but added, 'In my own time'

Her parents were a different matter. She wanted to let them know that all their troubles were over, longed to hear their delight as she told them . . . but something, some instinct born of caution, held her back. As Rik had said about his father, she told herself, in my own time I'll tell them.

There was in her luggage a dress which she had included in case, in the course of her job, she would have to follow her quarry to social functions. Sliding the dress from its hanger, she held its smooth scarlet brilliance against her.

As a colour, it was for her an unfamiliar choice. She had bought it on impulse with the advance on salary which Raymond Steele had given her. Seeing her attired in its clinging folds, Rik couldn't ignore her, that was for sure. Business deal or not, she was determined to look good to him.

Gold earrings matched the long gold chain her parents had given her in the years when their lives had been secure and trouble-free. After the shampoo and shower she had just taken, her hair felt soft and shining clean and, pulling on sandals which matched her dress and her lips, she felt she was ready for half a dozen Rik Steeles, let alone one.

'Where are we going?' she asked a little breathlessly as she settled herself into the passenger seat in Rik's sleek red car.

'To a hotel some way upstream. The Rushing River, it's called.'

'I supposed they know you there,' she commented with a provocative smile. 'I've yet to find a place where the great Rik Steele is *not* known.'

He cast amused and faintly provoked—eyes in her direction. 'You've got a lot to learn, Miss Hart, about Rik Steele.'

'A man of many sides.'

'Oh, yes,' he said, half under his breath. 'And no, they don't know me at the Rushing River.'

You could hear the roar of the weir even as you entered the foyer, Jan noticed. The lounge, with its floor-to-ceiling windows curving in a wide bay, provided a grand view of the sweep of the dancing, swirling water.

As Rik looked casually around, Jan sipped her aperitif and studied the menu, but found her eyes wandering constantly to the river scene beyond the wide-flung glass doors. Something about it drew, yet scared her, the distant roar, the relentless cascade, and a shiver took her by surprise.

They were seated opposite one another at a secluded table, and during the course of the meal she covertly admired the man who, she marvelled, had so unexpectedly become her husband-to-be. In his dark suit, the deep red tie a tasteful contrast, he looked urbane and broad-shouldered and impossibly handsome. And top to toe the man of business he had promised to become.

Elbows on the table, chin on his clasped hands, Rik contemplated her. 'You're looking at me,' he remarked, 'as if you've never seen me before.'

'I haven't,' was her breathy answer, 'not the man who's sitting opposite me now. Where's the tough-looking boatbuilder, the man with the bronzed torso wielding a hammer I watched the other day across the river? The "couldn't give a click of the fingers" host of the party I gatecrashed?'

'He's not far away, Janetta.' Rik leaned back and his face went into shadow, the flame from the candle in the silver holder casting a flickering light over the sparkling white of his shirt beneath the tailored jacket. 'Tell me something. Which of those men would you like to marry?'

How could she confess, I love them both so much I don't care which? So she shook her head, pretending puzzlement.

'The brawny guy in the dusty jeans,' he persisted, topping up her glass with the champagne which had accompanied their meal, then giving himself a refill, 'who shares a pint and a ploughman's with his mates, or the man of position and power, with a cheque-book that pours as much money into your purse as it can hold without spilling?'

Jan looked down at the plate that had held the expensive and exotic-tasting sweet, of which she had enjoyed every mouthful.

'That's a loaded question,' she pretended to prevaricate, 'and you know it. I think,' her eyes flicked up, and down, 'I think I liked the brawny guy an awful lot. He had rough cheeks in the evening, and even in the morning the razor hadn't really been give enough time by its owner to clear all the stubble away.'

Her companion lifted his glass to his lips, but his expression stayed hidden.

'His twin,' she moved her half-filled wineglass in a careful circle, 'his twin I find a terrible enigma. He's still a stranger,' she added in a whisper. 'I haven't——' a sip of wine moistened her lips, 'I haven't spend a night in his bed, have I?'

She gave him a shy, darting glance and he came forward out of the shadow into the candle's flirting flame.

'That, Janetta,' he replied, his voice low and husky, 'can be remedied.' His long lashes hid the expression in his eyes, but the candlelight threw the taut planes of his face into prominence.

'It wasn't——' Jan cleared her throat, 'it wasn't an invitation.'

'Where my fiancée's concerned, I don't need one.'

Her eyes encountered his at last. 'Is that an announcement of your intention? Because——' She shook her head.

'You're saying "no"?'

'Why shouldn't I?' she challenged. 'Our marriage will only be a business deal with no sentiment involved. Won't it?'

'So after marriage you intend to keep me out of your bed? You really expect me to remain celibate, banned even from the room my wife occupies? You honestly think you could get away with that?'

There was that tone again, the one that came from nowhere and held an authority that would plainly brook no denial. It hadn't come from the long-limbed, lithe-bodied Rik Steele, who laughed and joked and took life easily in his riverside home.

It had come from the man who, cold-bloodedly and calculatedly, had made this marriage deal with her and who, with his direct and worldly gaze, put a kind of electric current into her veins and made her nerve-ends sizzle and sting.

What kind of being had she, Frankenstein-like, brought into existence with her successful mission to persuade this man to agree to his father's wishes? When she had first met him, on his own ground, among his own friends, he had seemed easy to know, his thoughts and actions not entirely unpredictable.

But there was something about this man he had turned into that made her quiver inside, set her nerves on edge—and yet excited her beyond belief. He pulled her like a magnet, yet she knew she would never know tranquillity of mind again if she allowed him to pull her irreversibly into his orbit. What, for heaven's sake, had she done in bringing this side of him to life?

CHAPTER SEVEN

DESPITE the warmth of the restaurant, with its ruby-shaded lighting and its carpets and curtains to match, Jan's skin prickled with a cold fear.

'Do I mean to keep you from my bed?' she repeated his question. 'Yes, Rik.' She did not know how she found the strength to give such an answer, especially as it was in truth the very last thing she wanted to do. 'For me, the act of loving must have love as its springboard to give it depth and meaning. It's not in my nature to respond with passion to a man I——' she moistened her lips to allow the lie to be uttered, 'I don't have any feeling for.'

'Have no fear, my love,' drawled Rik, 'I'll ensure that you feel for me. Oh, yes,' his voice deepened, 'make no mistake, you'll dance to my tune. And the tune I play will be a sweet one, I promise.'

'But there won't be any love between us!' she cried from her depths. Then, embarrassed, she looked around her, hoping desperately that the other guests hadn't heard her outburst. None had, it seemed, and she stared at Rik, only to encounter his amusement at her emotional response.

'That's too bad, Janetta.' He leaned back, withdrawing into the shadows again. 'You knew the score when you agreed to our arrangement. Or were you really so naïve that you thought you could operate a "hands off" policy towards me throughout our married life? Especially,' his voice grew softly sensual, 'when you were offering me, along with our deal, a beautiful face and a seductive body?'

'All the same,' she answered, flustered by his outrageously flattering description of her, for of course she wasn't that attractive, 'when I slept in your bed, and I asked you to stop, you did. Which surprised me, because of what I'd heard about you.'

'Such as?' came coldly out of the shadows.

'Woman after woman——'

'And you believed it?' She was without doubt treading on dangerous ground.

'N-not after you held back when I asked you to.'

'Thanks for that,' he commented sarcastically.

'Just one woman,' Jan ventured to add. 'Nadia Beech.'

If she thought she might draw him on the subject, she found she was mistaken. He did not react in any way. Nor could she read his eyes, since he kept them hidden.

'Was she,' Jan probed against her better judgement, 'the married woman you said a marriage between us would keep at bay?'

The question remained unanswered since the waiter materialised. Dispensing the coffee, he left a dish of petits fours on the table. Absentmindedly, Jan pushed one of them into her mouth.

Rik leant forward. 'When I held back,' he remarked disconcertingly, watching the movement of her jaws as she demolished the tiny biscuit, 'it was because I had no right whatsoever to go on against your wishes. With my ring on your finger, no such barrier will exist.'

'If I—if I say "no", you'll make quite sure it doesn't exist, won't you?' she prevaricated. 'That barrier, I mean.'

His eyes glinted. 'At the first opportunity.'

'And if I say "yes", I know enough about you now to be quite sure you'll just set about demolishing it regardless.'

Rik's head went back in laughter, the candle flame darting madly at the disturbance of the air.

'Gotcha!' he quipped, covering her hand, picking up a petit four with the other and reaching across the table to pop it into her mouth. Then he selected one for himself.

There was about him at that moment, Jan thought with a zigzag of excitement, a lightning glimpse of the old Rik. Which brought her right back to the reason for their meeting each other in the first place.

She hated introducing the subject, but it couldn't be avoided any longer. 'Rik, we have to tell your father. About everything.'

He grew serious, his eyes cooling down. 'Tomorrow.'

'But Rik, why not tonight? It's not late, there's still time to ring——'

'Let's go.' His whole manner had hardened. He rose, coming round to ease back her chair.

The long drive to Rik's house was filled with taped music. Listening, Jan closed her eyes and tried to free the tension that was building up with every turn of the wheel.

In the driveway, Rik switched on the car's interior light. Turning her face towards him, he eased down the fur jacket that swung from her shoulders.

'Lady in red,' he said softly, eyeing her shape, 'you've got that certain something that gets a man's reflexes going. There's beauty, but more than that, there's——'

With a smothered exclamation, he hauled her closer and placed his mouth on hers, his hands smoothing her shoulders, her arms, her throat. When a palm brushed past her breasts, then returned to hold them possessively, they burgeoned in response. A gasp escaped her, parting her lips and allowing him all the access to their moist sweetness that he wanted.

Releasing her at last, but not completely relinquishing his hold, he looked into her glowing face. 'Besides being beautiful,' he commented, stroking the fur that lay behind her across the seat, 'my fiancée has expensive tastes.'

'Not mine,' she murmured, 'borrowed from my mother.'

'Take it, dear,' her mother had insisted. 'Your father won't mind, although he bought it for me. It holds so many happy memories, it hurts. I won't need it any more. We don't get invited out these days . . .'

'This chain?'

'A twenty-first birthday present from my parents.'

Releasing her, Rik raised his eyebrows. 'Comfortable middle-class upbringing you've had, by the sound of it?'

It was a question to which Jan could only nod in answer. What she couldn't add was, that's all in the past. They're almost destitute . . . but now, thanks to you and the money you've given me, I'll be able to do something about it.

'I can see,' he was saying, 'that I'd better provide for their daughter in the manner to which she's become accustomed, or else. Hm?' He ran a hard-skinned finger over her mouth. His love of everything to do with boats had plainly left its mark. To Jan's consternation, she wanted to put that hand to her lips, then nuzzle its tanned hair-sprinkled back to her cheek.

Her wayward thoughts confused her so much, she only just caught the drift of his comment. 'You must take me to meet them soon.'

Rik, meet her parents? It made her agreement to marry him so much more real —and more daunting. Could she go through with it? A loveless marriage—on Rik's part, at least? For her parents' sake, she told herself she would have to.

Her smile in response was strained, but he didn't seem to notice. Getting out, he went round to her door. 'Come on in. We're home.'

'Home', he called it. His it might be, she thought, following him, but it would take months, even years, for her to feel it was her home too. What a difference it would make if only he loved her . . .

In the living-room, he turned her towards him. A smile pulled at his mouth, eyes narrowing as they homed in on each of her features. 'Do you have to be so bloody desirable? I want you, Jan,' he declared, his voice low and husky.

Her gaze dropped to his bright tie, then her finger pressed one by one the buttons on the startling whiteness of his shirt. Did *he* have to look so handsome and distinguished in his formal clothes? 'Do you——' she swallowed, 'do you consider you have the right to ''want me''—any

more now than the night we shared the same bed
but you held back? Just proposing doesn't give it
to you, does it?'

'You're holding out until the ring's in place, are
you?' he growled.

'If I——' her forefinger outline the lapels of his
jacket, 'if I waited for your love, I'd wait for ever,
wouldn't I?' She hoped he had not picked up the
unintentional note of sadness which she had caught
in her own voice.

Rik's eyelids drooped. 'I never allow sentiment
to intrude into my business deals,' he replied
crisply. Leaving her, he crossed the room, sorting
through his collection of recorded music,
discarding his jacket on the way.

Watching the breadth of his back, the way his
shirt tautened with every fluid movement, Jan
wondered how she could have even entertained the
idea that she had touched his softer side. Because
he didn't have one, did he?

And could she have had it stated more
plainly—the commitment without the love? Oh,
Timothy, she thought, if you knew my
predicament now, after the final quarrel that
parted us, how you'd laugh and repeat what you
said on that last day—that I'd brought it all on
myself by seeing everything through a romantic
haze . . .

Rik set the hi-fi equipment going and the sound
was tender and sweet, but Jan found that its
coaxing melodies did not diffuse the tension which
had built up in her all evening. Through the glass
doors she stared into the black velvet night,
jumping violently as Rik's arms wrapped around
her waist from behind.

'Hush,' he murmured, nuzzling her ear, 'why so nervous? I may have thrown out my father's messengers in the past, but I've never eaten them for breakfast. Nor swallowed them as a nightcap.' Lips against her throat, he whispered, 'Dance with me.'

Pressed back against him, Jan tried to match her steps to his, but her legs were stiff and unco-operative. She told herself she couldn't afford to let them be otherwise. The spell he was weaving round her had to be resisted at all costs. Even if she had lost her heart, she mustn't lose her head, especially as Rik's was so very firmly on his shoulders.

His arms moved up, wrapping around her breasts, and a shudder ran through her. 'Let yourself go, Jan-ett-a,' he urged, seductively drawing out her name. 'My arms are strong. They won't let you down. Put your trust in me, all your life I'll be there . . .' The words were barely distinguishable above the magic sounds in the air.

Yes, physically, she acknowledged, if not emotionally, he'd be her back-up. She knew about his muscle power. Hadn't she glimpsed from across the river his arms at work? Hadn't the strength of them rescued her from drowning?

Now they were doing the opposite, impelling her down, down into the water again, water so deep and so swift that no one could help her, least of all Rik Steele. She was caught up in the currents of her love for him, swept away, floundering and going down, never to surface again . . .

The music was bewitching her, curling like drifting smoke around her emotions. Rik had lowered the lights, and moonlight crept in through the uncurtained windows.

When he turned her, she was limp with longing for him, her arms linking around his neck, while his hands imprisoned her hips against his.

'Janetta?' he murmured in that special way he had with her name. Looking up, eyes languorous and limpid, Jan encountered his mouth meeting hers head-on. All through the kiss they kept on dancing. As the rhythm manipulated her limbs, invoking smouldering desires, she thought she would die of love for him.

The music stopped and they stood, still embracing, the kiss hardening now, his mouth more intrusive and insistent.

'Janetta,' she heard his whisper, 'I want you—tonight.' He half pushed her from him. 'Go up. I'll follow.'

'No!' She never knew how she managed to defy him. 'I don't want you——' Without love, she'd been going to say. Why not? a voice cried inside her. This is all you'll ever get from him, lust and calculated passion.

'What did you say?' Ice-cold eyes held hers.

'I said "no", Rik.' There was anguish mixed with the defiance. If she let him make love to her, he'd guess . . . he wasn't stupid. He'd know how much she loved him. Then he'd laugh at her for her weakness, for her stupidity, *for bringing sentiment into a business deal*. And turn to Nadia for escape from her clinging, unsophisticated arms.

Roughly he put her aside and strode past, up the stairs like the wind, slamming his bedroom door.

Scrambling from the bed, she stood at the window, her slender figure drenched in moonlight. She could not sleep, her thoughts would not let her. Not only that, her body cried out for Rik's touch so desperately that she almost had to restrain herself from running along the corridor and saying, 'It's "yes", Rik. . .*please.*'

When the door creaked, she thought she was back in bed and dreaming. He had come to her! He stood in the doorway, the light from behind him outlining his height and broad physique. The door swung closed and he moved towards her. Her heart lurched, but she turned her back on him, fearful of giving away her delight at his coming.

'Janetta?' His voice had lost its harshness, and when his hands came to rest on her shoulders she shivered because she knew that this side of him was something she would not, either now or ever, be able to resist.

'Yes?'

'Turn around.'

Bereft of any will of her own, she obeyed, staring up into his moon-shaded face. His eyes were in shadow, but the angles contained in his facial structure assumed a mystery that set her heart pounding, her limbs turning to water even though he had hardly touched her. He wore a belted black kimono which emphasised his masculinity, the way it wrapped around him suggesting that he wore nothing beneath it. Taking a glinting object from a pocket, he commanded, 'Give me your hand. Your *left* hand.'

The ring he slid on to her wedding finger glowed in the moon's shining light. It was a perfect fit. It seemd to be of antique design, and she tried without sucess to distinguish its stones.

'Rubies, diamonds, moonstones and a pearl or

two,' Rik told her. 'It was my mother's. After a pause, he added, 'It's yours now.'

He was giving her his mother's ring, when it must mean so much to him? 'Rik, are you sure? It—it's not as though you love me. A business deal, you said——'

'As you're my wife-to-be, Janetta, it's yours now.' He had spoken so decisively, she knew there would be no arguing with him. Lifting her hand, he put it to his lips.

'Rik,' she gazed up at him, her voice wavering, 'what can I say?' Impulsively, she reached up, pulling his head low enough for her lips to touch his cheek.

What she had not anticipated was the speed of his response, encircling her and pulling her against him. His mouth forced hers open and she knew beyond doubt that, with his ring on her finger, any attempt at refusal on her part would be overridden by him. Nothing now would prevent him from taking what he wanted.

And this time she knew that she wanted it too—wanted his body close, wanted *him* with a longing that frightened her. Once in his arms, she was sure she would not be able to disguise her feelings, and their 'business deal' would surely end right there. Rik wanted her as his wife, she reminded herself, only as a 'condition' of his return to his father's life, and as a barrier to other men's wives. Hadn't he said so?

'Rik, no . . .' She twisted her throat in an effort to escape his burning trail of kisses. 'I don't——'

'But I do.' His sharp teeth tugged at her earlobe. 'And I will. Now I've got the right I didn't have the night you shared my bed, you don't have any power of refusal.'

'But I do! I could say you must wait for our wedding . . .'

Wrapping her around him as if he were grafting her on to his body, he put back his head and laughed. 'You can tell me to wait as much as you like—in fact, if we were marrying tomorrow, I might—just—give in to your whim. But it won't happen that soon and I'm not a patient man. It's something you'll learn——'

'In our *intimate business dealings*, you mean,' she taunted, delaying the moment of surrender for as long as she could.

Rik laughed again, the moonlight catching his jawline and the strong cords of his throat, turning him into an exciting, if slightly menacing, stranger. Because he *was* a stranger, she told herself—Rik Steele, the lover, the side of him which she'd never encountered before.

'I paid a substantial price for you, my lady,' he muttered against her mouth, 'so substantial it gives me the power to dictate terms——'

'If you think you're going to *dictate* to me,' she retorted, stiffening in his arms, 'then think again, because——'

Her defiance, her physical resistance, seemed to roughen his feelings. He tugged down the shoulder straps of her nightdress, then his lips made heated contact, his teeth implanting minute nips on her skin. When she yelped and tried to struggle in his forceful hold, he merely tightened it and ran his tongue-tip over the tiny marks his teeth had made, his head moving down with the filmy fabric until his lips found the bare flesh of her breasts. It was uncharted territory for his mouth and his tongue, and Jan's head fell back as she gasped with the pleasure the intimate contact was giving her.

When her nightdress lay in a heap at her feet, Rik held her away, looking her over, his eyes glinting in the moon's silvered light.

'Take off my robe,' he commanded softly. 'Now,' as she hesitated. 'I want the feel of you against me, your soft curves pressing against my flesh. *Will* you do as I say?' There was an edged kind of urgency in his voice, the impatience he had spoken of coming through.

'Not——' Jan took a breath, 'not until I've told you, Rik . . . there may be consequences. And,' she moistened her lips, 'you wouldn't want a child to bind you to me, would you? That was never mentioned as part of our deal.'

His face, partly in shadow, told her nothing.

'And', she went on, 'when one day I do have a baby, I want it to be by the man I love . . .'

The flash that tore across his eyes revealed the extent of his anger at her statement. 'Have no fear, my *loving* fiancée,' he grated, 'I'll take care of that side of things—this time.'

Her words seemed to have banished all his consideration and tenderness. His hold on her hardened, his lips and hands roaming her body, uncaring where they settled, demanding response. He swept her up, lifting her high, then dropping her on to the bed. Shedding his robe, he covered her form with his.

Her entire being leapt to throbbing life at the intimacy of his touch, and she found herself arching towards him, twisting under the relentless arousal of his hands. When she thought she would die with wanting him, he grasped her hips and lifted her, making a path for himself into her enclosing warmth. She cried out his name, trying to keep to herself the thrust of pain he had inflicted.

But he'd realised . . . 'My God,' she heard him whisper, but he did not stop. Keeping up the heady rhythm of his possession, his movements gentled, but only a little, his hands turning to stroking and to persuasion, his mouth teasing, caressing and seducing.

When she thought there could be no greater pleasure, he took her with him, higher and higher into the midst of a golden cloud where the world ceased to matter and nothing existed except their complete and total oneness.

For a long time they lay, bodies entangled, then she whispered, 'I'm sorry, Rik, if—if you were disappointed.' He merely growled and moved his head to rest against her breasts, nuzzling their softness.

She delighted in the intimate feel of him against her, and her arms wrapped themselves around him, her hand stroking his hair. She thought she had loved him before, but knew that it had been as nothing compared with her feeling for him now.

'An untouched woman, Janetta—surely in these "enlightened" days is a prize in almost any culture. How come? I can't believe the chances didn't arise.'

'Of course they did.' How could she tell him, I was waiting for the right man? 'There was Timothy. But I believe in marriage.'

'And he didn't?'

'Right.'

'So marriage was your price. Still is, isn't it? By offering to marry you, I got the girl.' Rik's bronzed shoulders shrugged. 'I'm not complaining.' He lay down with a grunt of contentment and pulled her on top of him so that their limbs entwined, hip fitting into hip, breast brushing chest. 'What would you do, my bewitching little go-between,' his half-smile teased, but his eyes weren't laughing, 'if I changed my mind about my father's request and walked out on you now?'

The thought was like being pierced by an arrow, but she summoned a smile. 'Mm,' her eyes sparked and her fingernails ran over his roughening cheeks as if she were filing them to finer points, the better to scratch him with, 'maybe I'd sue.'

'No such thing as breach of promise these days, thank God. Try again. And there's been no contract signed between us, nothing in writing,' he taunted, smiling. 'I could walk away right now and end it. It's only what they used to call a "gentleman's agreement" between us, anyway—if you can call someone like me a "gentleman".'

'Mm.' She pretended to reflect, then teased, 'How about—take up with another man?'

To her dismay, he took her seriously, his eyes darkening dangerously, his jaw growing rigid. He rolled her beneath him and put himself on top of her, his mouth coming down in a wide-lipped merciless kiss. His hands grew rough on her body, making her writhe and gasp and open herself to him with an abandonment she revelled in, yet feared—that he should be able to wield so much power over her, making her yield to his every command.

When he took her again, she moaned with the ecstasy of his total possession, giving and giving to his relentless demands until the stars in the sky seemed to burst into the room and explode into a million diamonds all around.

'Don't,' he rasped against her mouth, 'don't ever let me hear you speak that way again. Do you hear?' His hand wrapped around her throat and he stared into her brilliant, love-dazzled eyes, keeping her pliant body pinned beneath him as she whispered a breathless 'yes'.

It was morning when Jan stirred, stretching her arms luxuriously, eager to greet the new day.

Rolling on to her side, she reached out—to find an empty space. Rik had gone! Had he, after all, fulfilled his joking threat to walk out on her? Or was he taking a shower?

'Rik,' she called, an unintentional note of panic in her voice, 'where are you?'

He was seated by the window, his back to her, casually dressed and freshly clean. On his lap was a file of papers, in his hand a pen poised to make notes.

The smile he threw over his shoulder held mockery. 'A voice crying in the wilderness,' he commented. 'How can I resist a beautiful women in distress?'

Jan's heart overflowed with love for him, her legs under the covers moving restlessly, wanting his limbs back beside her for hers to entangle with.

'Without you to fill the empty space beside me,' she remarked with smiling provocation, 'this bed's not just a wilderness, it's a barren waste.'

He laughed. 'One ravished siren learning fast how to get her lover to seduce her all over again!'

'Is there something wrong with that?' she asked

with mock innocence. 'I'm wearing your ring now, which you said from the start was the "key" to the bedroom door. So——?'

She stretched out her arms to him, but he did not move, just looked at her enigmatically.

'You,' she shot at him, angered and embarrassed by his refusal to come to her, 'are the absolute epitome of "businessman at work" following a night's lustful dalliance with your chosen bedmate. A one-night stand, in fact.' She rolled on to her face, upset by his apparent detachment after all those hours in each other's arms. He was treating her as if she were really part of a business deal. 'You're—you're insulting me, Rik,' she said, her face muffled by the pillow.

He smile faintly, but seemed unmoved by her challenge. She'd get a positive response out of him, she resolved, no matter how long it might take. No man, she vowed, let alone her fiancé, was going to treat her with contempt.

'Keeping rigidly to the terms of our engagement?' she taunted again, lifting her face from the pillow. 'Relaxation over, strictly business during daylight hours?'

Rik swung fully round, hooded eyes threatening, but some of the papers on his lap slid off and he bent to retrieve them, cursing. She laughed, knowing she had aroused him at last.

'You,' he said narrow-eyed, 'are behaving like a mistress. If that's what you want, OK, the marriage is off. From now on you're a kept woman, to use the old-fashioned term—*my* kept woman.'

After the erotic pleasures of the night, the happiness she had discovered in his arms, Jan found it difficult to accept his mood swing—and his pointed barbs.

'Why——' her lip quivered, 'why are you being so—so unpleasant to me this morning? You said such wonderful things in the night. If I've provoked you now, it was only because I—I resented being treated like a clause in that business contract we made between us. You're my lover now, Rik, which means something to me, even if it doesn't to you . . .'

'OK, I'm sorry, I'm sorry.' He rose, putting the papers aside, walking up and down. 'A few days ago I contacted a family friend who's also a business associate of my father's. At my request, he sent me a few relevant facts and figures which I've just been looking through. Steele Construction, my father's company, is in a bloody awful mess. No wonder the message was of the "all is forgiven, for God's sake come home" variety! I should have looked before I leapt.'

After all they had shared, it was too much! 'Before proposing to me, you mean,' Jan blurted out, profoundly upset by all that his statement implied, 'before leaping into my bed and demanding your rights as my husband-to-be.'

Pushing aside the bedcover, she realised with a shock that she was still naked. Rik stopped being preoccupied, his eyes homing in on her body. Flustered by his narrowed, assessing gaze, she grabbed his kimono and slid into it, gathering her clothes.

'Feel free, *Mr Steele*,' she cried, 'to walk out of here, back to the life you enjoy so much. *And Nadia Beech, the woman you love!*'

'Who said?'

'No one, but I know.'

'You do, do you? Womanly intuition, is it?'

'I just know, so you can stop sneering. She's the one you really want, isn't she?'

Almost in the bathroom, she turned on him again.

'You've had the d-doubtful pleasure of violating a virgin and I've had the b-benefit of being d-deflowered by an experienced man and a g-great lover. Big deal for me!' she stormed. 'Also, since you haven't yet told your father, he need never know, need he, how near you came to agreeing to his request? Therefore he won't be disappointed. And don't worry, you'll get your cheque back just as soon as I can find it. Goodbye, Rik. It's been n-nice knowing you——'

He was across the room and into the bathroom in front of her. Before she could draw breath, he had stripped her of covering and was pushing her under the warm shower. Moments later, naked himself, he stepped beside her, taking her in his arms and, as the water rained down, kissed her until her knees almost buckled beneath her.

Then systematically he set about arousing her all over again, kissing and caressing each intimate corner and secret portion of her anatomy until every inch of her throbbed and ached for him. She heard herself cry, 'Rik, oh, Rik, take me again . . . I want you so much!'

'That's better,' he said, his voice like spurting gravel. Carrying her to the bed, he took immediate and thrusting possession, lifting her with him to heights of incomparable delight, joining her in an explosion of sheer, unbridled joy such as she had never experienced in her life before.

CHAPTER EIGHT

WAKING for the second time, Jan slowly became aware of being alone. The folder of papers had gone, as well as the man who had been scanning them. The sun had climbed higher, warming her bare skin as she lay in deep contentment.

Stirring reluctantly, she reached for her watch. It told her that she would be having a late breakfast. Rik, she surmised, had left for his beloved work, while the chance still remained for him to do it.

There was a telephone in the room, a thoughtful touch for the guests he invited for weekend parties . . . And she knew all about Rik Steele's parties, didn't she? If she knew the number of the boatyard she could ring him, tell him—what? How much she loved him? How happy he had made her? Don't be stupid, she told herself. Strictly business, wasn't it? Not a single word of love must be allowed to pass her lips. She closed her eyes. No, she wouldn't call him, not even just to say 'hello'.

But she could telephone her parents and give them the good news. They were overjoyed to hear it. It wasn't, however, at all easy convincing her mother that of course she was marrying for love!

'Oh, Mum,' Jan added, unable to keep the tears of happiness from her voice, 'your money troubles are over! I can't tell you know glad——'

'You're being entirely honest with me, darling? Penelope Hart queried uncertainly. 'You love this man you've chosen?'

'Madly,' Jan answered, without needing to cross her fingers because it was the truth she was telling.

Showering again, she selected a white linen pleated shirt and a matching open-necked sweater with a deep blue yacht motif, combing her fair hair around a face so flushed and vital she could scarcely recognise it as her own. Her eyes appeared bluer, her lips fuller and a deeper red. With a jump of her heartbeat she remembered Rik's bruising, binding kisses, and her tongue lightly touched her lips in sweet remembrance of the lovemaking.

The coffee she made for herself braced her tastebuds, but she was too full of happiness for food. In the night she had savoured the very essence of heaven, and its ambrosial richness would satisfy her bodily appetite for hours to come.

As she drank, the telephone rang. She tensed, half-rising to answer it, but the sound was cut off abruptly, telling her that Rik must be at work in his study and not at the boatyard as she had assumed.

Rinsing her cup, she wandered through the hallway, making for the garden. Rik's voice reached her from the near-distance. 'As I see it, Nadia,' he was saying, 'there's only one action I can take in the circumstances. It's the end for——'

He was talking to Nadia again!

Covering her ears, Jan ran the last few steps into the open air. *The end for us*, she was sure he had been going to say. She didn't want to hear the explanations and the regrets, the soothing words and lingering endearments. She wouldn't listen to him saying, 'So you want us to go on seeing each other, even though I'm tied to a wife? Well, OK, darling, but——'

She went where her feet took her, down to the river. Watching the driftwood floating by, she vowed that one day she would force Nadia Beech into second place in Rik's life.

It was mid-morning and the riverbanks were clear of boats. Night-time mornings had been abandoned; for the holiday-makers, now was the time of day for movement and exploration.

From out of the haze that held the promise of a fine day came the sound of raucous singing. Jan peered into the mist. Her ears told her who it was even before her eyes picked out the rowing boat in which he was drifting.

'Hi there, doorstep baby!' yelled Tony, waving a beer can and grinning. 'I thought you'd gone, walked out of my life. And without even kissing me goodbye!'

He drained the can, raising it high to fling it from him, but Jan shouted, 'Tony, don't! You'll pollute the river.'

To her surprise, Tony gave an exaggerated shrug and dropped the can into the boat, only to pick up another, peeling it open and swigging its contents. Then he gave a great hiccup and leaned back drunkenly.

'Tony, you've had enough,' Jan urged. 'You really shouldn't——'

'Why shouldn't I?' Tony demanded. 'Boss is out—gone missing, they said. Chasing a woman, probably.' He leant over to grab the mooring platform and hoisted himself on to it, the boat rocking as he levered himself up. Despite his drunken state, he had the presence of mind to grope for the mooring rope and wind it round the iron post. Pulling his unco-ordinated body up the slope, he grasped Jan to him, one arm around her waist while the other held her head to his shoulder. 'This,' he pronounced, his words slurred, 'is the woman I love. She——'

Jan struggled without success to free herself. 'Tony,' she said urgently, easing back her head, 'shouldn't you be at work?'

He half released her and stared into her eyes. 'Hey, golden girl, you look different. Who's been getting fresh with you? Tell me, and I'll smash his——' The truth dawned. 'No, it's not true,' he moaned, his words running into one another. 'That— that——' he mouthed a word under his breath, 'he hasn't got at you?' He read her face closely. 'He has, the lowdown rotten——!'

'Moore,' rasped a voice from behind them, 'you're fired!'

Tony forgot to remove his arms. Instead, they stiffened and Jan was imprisoned against him. 'Rik,' she implored over her shoulder, 'please don't——'

Rik looked scathingly from Jan to Tony. 'I can do what the hell I like,' he rasped, 'where my employees are concerned. Moore, get your hands of my wife-to-be and get the hell out of here!'

Tony's face drained. 'Your——' He glared at Jan. 'You've agreed to marry him? Say you haven't. Darling, a woman can let a man bed her these days without having to make it legal.'

A hand reached out from behind and sent him spinning, that hand catching Jan's arm and pulling her bruisingly away.

She bit her lip but kept her cry of pain to herself. Tony found the vertical again and challenged, 'Why are you firing me, boss? What harm is there in taking a little row——'

'One,' Rik counted on his fingers, eyes blazing, 'absent without leave. Two, taking the firm's property——' he indicated the rowing-boat with the Dancing River motif on its hull, 'without permission, and three, drunk in working hours.'

'But, Rik—hell, I need the job! I need the money. How'm I going to manage without it?'

'You should have thought that out before you decided to play while the cat was away.'

'My God,' exclaimed Tony, 'call yourself a cat? I'd call you a tiger—with the teeth of a crocodile!' He hiccuped, then looked gloomily at Jan. 'Hope you don't regret it, golden girl. That guy'll make your life hell. I wouldn't wish him on any woman, least of all you. See you some time.'

He ambled away, weaving up the slope of the lawn and round the side of the house towards the road. The empty rowing-boat bobbed about, the remaining beer cans clattering against each other.

'So what were you doing?' Rik enquired icily. 'Comforting a drunken sailor?'

'Why did you have to fire him?' countered Jan. 'Couldn't you have given him another chance?'

'He's had it. It's crunch time now for him. He's out of the firm, and that's it.'

Jan stared at the rowing-boat as it rode the river's ripples. 'I didn't throw myself into Tony's arms just now,' she said. 'He grabbed me. It upset him to discover——' She fingered her ring, wishing she hadn't spoken.

'And you were consoling him for his "great loss" and promising him a reward if he hung around in dark places——'

She flung from him furiously, but he caught her

and jerked her to him, pressing her against his hard hips and covering her mouth with his. 'No man,' he muttered, lifting his head at last, 'no man so much as touches my wife-to-be from now on, understand?'

He kissed her again, this time until she bent backwards under the pressure, but he showed no mercy, following her down until she fought for breath. When he had finished with her he jerked her up, his arms dropping away, but the feelings he had aroused in her of wanting and longing for him caused her to cling and raise a heated face to his, full of passion fighting with anger.

His possessiveness both thrilled and frightened her. 'I refuse to let you dictate what I can and can't allow other people to do after we're married. Get up to date, Rik, we're living in a modern age where——'

'No man, do you hear?' he snarled, his cheekbones prominent as his hard jaw thrust forward.

Of course she wouldn't even contemplate allowing any man the privileges she would allow him as her husband, nor even as her fiancé—but she was darned if she was going to tell him that out loud.

'You don't love me,' she snapped, her head back, eyes flashing. 'You never will. That wasn't included in our arrangements, was it? All you want of me is to follow you around like a little lapdog, wagging my tail at every opportunity and generally nuzzling up to your business cronies and guests.'

'You'll "nuzzle up to" no one but me,' Rik returned, lips twitching.

'Rik——' Her breath caught in her lungs and

came out jerkily. 'Oh, Rik,' she whispered, 'I'm mad——' Her teeth clamped down over the words her lips were about to speak. 'Mad about you,' she'd so nearly said. She had almost given herself away to him, letting him know she was his and his alone . . .

'Mad to have agreed to our engagement, you mean?' he rasped.

Jan was shaking her head when the distant peal of the doorbell broke into their quarrel.

Imperfect timing on Nadia's part for once, she reflected cynically, watching Rik stride away. Nadia, making her entrance at the start of a disagreement which, given enough mileage, might have terminated the engagement, putting Rik Steele back within her reach.

The murmur of voices that reached Jan as she entered the house told her that Rik's visitor was male. The unexpected guest seemed to have arrived in anything but a conciliatory mood. Was it Tony, she wondered with dismay, come to plead for his job back?

When her ears told her the identity of the newcomer, her heart began to hammer. Raymond, followed closely by his son, entered the living-room, and Jan saw that he was shaking.

'Jan, I told you to leave here,' he said, his voice gruff. 'On the phone I pleaded with you to come back at once.' His hand came to rest on her shoulder. 'As your employer, Jan, I insist——'

'Raymond——' she broke in, then paused, glancing uncertainly at Rik, aware that what she had to tell his father might come as a shock, 'you're not my employer any more.'

Raymond's hand dropped away, eyes puzzled.

Then his eyes widened. 'There could be only one circumstance in which you would have left my employment.' He turned to his son. 'Does this mean you're coming back?' he asked incredulously. 'This time, Richard, you're——' he seemed hoarse with disbelief, 'this time you're going to answer my call? My dear son,' his voice appeared to crack, 'I—I hardly know what to say!'

'Thank your messenger,' came Rik's clipped reply.

'You mean Jan?' Raymond's voice was tender. 'I knew from the moment I set eyes on her that she was——'

'Different?' Why, Jan wondered, did he sound so cynical?

'Exactly. But,' Raymond frowned, 'she told me on the phone that she'd failed in her mission.'

'I—er—changed my mind,' Rik replied. 'You chose well this time, Father. I found it impossible to resist this particular go-between's—persuasive technique.'

Had Raymond picked up the thinly veiled sarcasm? It seemed not, since his eyes still rested warmly on Jan.

'Are you well?' Rik asked coolly. As if he were questioning a mere passing acquaintance, Jan thought despairingly.

'Er——' Raymond glanced down, then back at his son. 'Much better, Richard, for having you back in my life. You don't know how glad . . . You called Jan a "go-between".' He gave a short, indulgent laugh. 'She's much more than that. I owe you money, my dear. You don't know how glad I'll be to part with it to you.'

'You owe her nothing,' Rik replied crisply. 'I've settled the account.'

'No, no, you don't understand, Richard.' The lines of his father's face crinkled gently. 'I'm talking about the lump sum I arranged to pay Jan on completion of——'

'Her mission? She told me about it. I asked her the amount, then doubled it. She was,' Rik's quick, secret glance was unmistakably sensual, 'worth it.'

Jan blushed, then her heart raced with anger. Was that how he *still* regarded her? As a woman whose 'services' he had paid for?

There was a puzzled silence. Raymond seemed afraid to break it.

'She accepted something else too,' said Rik. 'Janetta.' His hand extended and, as if she were hypnotised, Jan went towards it, allowing its warm strength to grasp her, pulling her closer. 'She accepted my proposal of marriage, Father.'

It took a few moments for the words to make an impact. Then it was as if a hand grenade had exploded at Raymond's feet. The colour drained from his face, his arms stiffened at his sides, fists clenched. For a handful of seconds he seemed to sway.

'Rik, your father——' Jan made to go to him, but Rik would not let her.

'Do you need a doctor, Father?' he asked. 'Are you taking any medication?'

Raymond slumped to a chair, ignoring his son's concern. 'Tell me it's not true, Jan,' he whispered hoarsely.

'It's true,' Rik answered for her. 'It was the condition I made for agreeing to your request. You must surely admit,' he added, not without a touch of cynicism, 'that a man of my age, taking on the position you want me to occupy, needs a woman at his side—a legally binding partnership. To counteract gossip, if nothing else.'

'You made this a condition? So,' Raymond's voice challenged, scoring a point, 'she agreed under duress? Which means she can't be held to it.'

Rik's eyes narrowed, swinging to Jan. 'If she reneges, I shall refuse your request.'

Raymond looked up then, holding Jan's eyes. 'There's no need for you to make this sacrifice, my dear. I shall carry on working, after all. My—my health—did I forget to tell you? It's not as good as it might be. But it will improve. The doctors will see me through.'

Then he looked at her, really looked, seeing the new happy knowledge in her eyes.

Rising, he shook with anger. 'My son,' he got out, 'I have to say it. You're a cold, calculating swine! You wasted no time, did you? You've taken her innocence. It was a rare and beautiful thing. And the tragedy is that to you the act meant nothing.'

Rik's jaw hardened, a muscle moving in his cheek, but to Jan's infinite sadness he did not deny his father's assertion. Had she really tried to fool herself that, for him, their lovemaking had meant something more than the passing satisfaction of a basic need?

Raymond's eyes swept to Jan. 'I warned you, my dear, against my son's ways with women. He has no mercy. And no heart, do you hear? He'll never love you, no matter how many times he takes you to bed. So break with Richard, Jan,' Raymond urged. 'Withdraw your agreement to become his wife.'

I love him, she wanted to cry out, letting the whole world know, but she stifled the confession, pushing it back into the strong box in her mind where it had to stay for ever.

Rik lifted her left hand, making sure it caught his father's eye.

'You've given her *that* ring?' whispered Raymond, lifting incredulous eyes to his son's.

Rik dropped the hand and pocketed his own, head held at a challenging angle, almost as if, Jan thought, he were daring his father to object.

What was this strange, wordless discussion they were having? she wondered. Then something snapped inside her. She'd played a go-between for these two men long enough. 'I refuse to take any more!' she cried, her feet taking her to the door.

'Janetta!' Rik's hand shot out, but she took evasive action.

'Goodbye, Rik,' she choked. 'Thanks for—everything. Raymond, thank you too . . .'

He was beginning to sway, but she knew she had to leave, regardless of the consequences of her action. Some of her belongings, she told herself as she made for the stairs, she would pile into a case. The rest would have to stay.

Behind her in the hall, Rik rasped, 'If you go back on our marriage deal, I'll withdraw from my agreement to take over my father's job. What's more,' his eyes narrowed, his mouth curled, 'if you pack up and go, you'll forfeit that small fortune you've made out of me. So what's your answer?'

He'd trapped her! If she answered 'it's goodbye', not only would she lose him out of her life, she would be faced with the awful task of telling her parents she couldn't help them after all—after giving them a glimpse of their own private Promised Land. Yet, if she agreed not to leave, he would think the worst of her. Once again, she really had no choice.

'I'll stay,' she whispered hoarsely.

Contempt filled his eyes. 'That's my acquisitive, money-mad girl! I could see the pound signs doing a frenzied dance in those *innocent* blue eyes of yours while you pretended to consider the options.'

The telephone rang and he swung on his heel, leaving her without a backward glance.

Raymond reclined, eyes closed, in a garden chair a few feet from a rosebed massed with softly glowing blooms. Jan, seated near him on the grass, inhaled the heavy perfume and stared unseeingly at the newspaper. Still ringing in her ears, still mocking, were Rik's contemptuous words.

The day had dragged. She knew Rik had not left the house, because now and then she heard him speaking on the telephone. At one point, the doorbell had rung. She had been half-way to answering it when Rik forestalled her.

Nadia had stood radiant and smiling on the doorstep. 'Darling,' she'd said, 'you can't do without me, can you? When you called I was in the middle of a shower. You should have joined me there as I suggested. Rik darling,' she touched his arm, 'the business we could have done if you had!'

Over his shoulder Nadia had spied Jan, but her expression revealed that she had known all along that she'd had an audience. Then she had reached across and kissed Rik's cheek, a waft of expensive perfume touching even Jan's nostrils.

Turning abruptly, unable to stand any more of Nadia's clever taunts, Jan had turned and run. Nadia's tinkling laugh had rung out, and a door had closed on the sound.

Raymond looked pale, and Jan could not decide whether he was asleep or had been lulled to a deep tranquillity by the river's soothing sound, the swish of passing boats, the happy cries of children.

Her eyes returned to scan the newspaper. Idly she turned the pages. She had intended to miss the financial section, but the heading of a column caught her eye. 'Troubled Steele Engineering', it read, 'directors concerned . . . stagnation threatens . . . urgent need for new thinking . . . future bleak without fresh horizons to aim for . . .'

A noisy passing motor-launch brought Raymond's eyes open. Seeing Jan nearby, he stirred. 'Jan?' His hand came out.

Hastily closing the newspaper and putting it aside, she commented, 'I thought you were asleep.'

'Not really. I've been drifting. And thinking—or trying to. Will you come, Jan? Over here?'

Jan complied, settling herself at his feet. Raymond patted his knee. 'Rest your head, Jan, if you like.' She did so and, in an abstracted, paternal fashion, his hand stroked her hair.

The father's touch was gentler than the son's, but it wasn't gentleness she craved. It was the strong, masterful embrace she longed for of the man who had held and dominated her that morning. With all her heart she wished she were back in his arms, his probing lips on hers, his hands arousing a frantic desire in every tingling part of her . . . Oh, God, she thought, I love him so.

'I'll have to leave,' Raymond was saying slowly. 'Pleasant though this place is, I can't impose on my son for too long. He's agreed to my request. For that I must be thankful, more than thankful, but I'd give a fortune for his affection. When he told me that day that he wanted to break away and not come into the business, I suppose I should have been more understanding. But,' he shook his head, 'when a dream you've cherished for over twenty-five years is shattered before your eyes . . .' His sigh was deep and shaky.

Jan nodded, weeping inside for the father of the man she adored. We're in the same boat, she reflected sadly, Raymond and I. I'd give all I possessed, too, for even a little of that affection.

'There's a dear friend of mine,' Raymond went on. 'Celia Lacey, a widow—lives in Bedford. Any time I liked I could go and stay, she said.'

There was a long pause. Jan played with the blades of grass around her, tugging at them, then throwing them away.

Looking up, she saw across the river a forlorn figure walking along the towpath. His feet dragged, his pockets bulged with fisted hands. His eyes seemed drawn to hers and he glanced across, staring moodily, then moving on. Tony sacked, Jan thought, her heart following him. Why did Rik have to be such a hard man of business?

'Don't marry him,' urged Raymond, breaking into her thoughts.

'But I love him, Raymond. I——'

'No, no, you only think you do, because he's the first.' She was shaking her head against his knee, but he held it still. 'It's nothing but infatuation, believe me.'

'Father——' A step sounded behind them and Rik stood there, taking the scene.

'Forgive me for interrupting such a tender moment,' he drawled, turning to go. Hadn't he *any* understanding or sympathy where his father was concerned? Jan wondered sadly.

'Richard, stay! Jan was——' Raymond smiled down at the fair head resting against him, 'giving me comfort.'

'It gets monotonous,' Rik said grimly. Tony, he means, Jan thought with a spurt of anger.

Raymond straightened and Jan scrambled to her feet, smoothing her hair, shivering inside under Rik's cold stare.

Irrationally, her anger flared, against Raymond, who had been responsible for her being there at all, against Rik for stealing her heart. 'Will you excuse me?' she said.

'Unfortunately, no,' Rik rapped out. 'It's business I want to talk to my father about. You're going to be one of the family——' Jan's heart jolted at his unemotional statement and all that it implied, 'I might also need your assistance as a personal secretary.' He drew up a garden chair for her use. 'I take it you do have qualifications in that direction?'

'Yes, I do. Is this an interview?' she tossed at him, eyes flashing.

His eyes sparked at her impudence. 'Good,' he said. A cynical smiled pulled at his lips. 'I couldn't have chosen better. A wife-to-be with looks *and* ability.'

Crossing her legs, Jan rearranged her skirt, then coloured as Rik's reminiscent, very male stare lingered on her calves and ankles. Pretending a nonchalance she did not feel, she leaned back, her colour deepening under Rik's insolent inspection of her thrusting shape as her white sweater tightened with the action. Fleetingly, he noticed the yacht motif above her right breast, then eyed her narrowly as if suspecting that she had worn the top for his benefit.

Then his manner said back-to-business. 'I guess you're aware, Father,' he said, 'of the perilous state of Steele Construction?'

'Well aware, son.'

'It could come crashing.'

Raymond winced at the bluntness, but nodded. 'It's one of the reasons I wanted your help.'

'You realise there's virtually no cash flow? That all you're doing is servicing the interest on the bank loan you've got, not even reducing the capital?'

Tiredly, Raymond nodded.

'For a company to prosper, you need growth. I'm sure you'll agree.' Raymond agreed. 'But without finance to fund it, a company can only die. Agreed again? So, to obtain these funds, you need,' Rik pressed forefinger, with forefinger, 'profit, none of which I can trace in the company's books. Also another injection of capital——'

'Can't be done, Richard. I've tried.' Raymond stared in front of him.

'Then we'll have to try harder.'

'The bank said "no".'

'Enlarge your overdraft.'

'Do you think I haven't tried?' Raymond responded wearily.

'I'm beginning to understand,' Rik went on, his manner relenting, but only for a moment, 'your call to me for help. Debtors,' he went on briskly, 'must be tackled, cash owing to the company must be collected.'

'Have *you* ever tried squeezing money out of a stone?'

After the merest pause, Rik stated, 'My plan is to bring my own company under the Steele umbrella.'

Raymond's head jerked round. 'The firm's surely in a bad enough state, Richard, without adding to its troubles.'

'I could,' Rik said with a surprising mildness, 'take exception to that statement. But I won't. Steele & Mountford boatbuilding and design are doing very nicely, thank you. Not just nationally, but world-wide. Dancing River Seagoers and Waterfloats are in great demand.'

'Dancing River? That's *your* company?' Raymond exclaimed.

Rik smiled faintly. 'Good grief, if even my head-in-the-sand father has heard of it, it must be on the up an up!'

Raymond was ready with a rebuke for his son's mild disrespect, but he smiled instead. Just like the old days, Jan could almost hear him thinking. 'Financial pages. I see it mentioned frequently.'

There was a distant crunch of tyres on gravel, the sound of a familiar horn making its owner's presence known. At once Rik was on his feet.

Jan's head jerked away, tears springing and blending with the river's flowing movement. 'Go on, go to your woman,' she murmured under her breath.

Hardened fingertips pulled her head round, but she closed her eyes. 'What did you say?'

'I said,' her lips scarcely opening to mouth the

words, 'your woman wants you.' A tear escaped, but she dashed it away, adding through her teeth, 'You should make "stud" your middle name!'

'Janetta!' Rik said roughly.

Her eyes came open, intending to challenge, to say, I don't care a darn for you, but something in them must have touched him, since he bent and brushed her mouth with his. Annoyed by his apparent attempt to placate, and by the treachery of her lips in accepting his kiss without protest, she lifted her chin free of his hold.

The imperious horn summoned him again.

'I see you dance to *her* tune,' Jan taunted to his retreating back. He came to a halt, half turned, but changed his mind. Jan let out the breath she had drawn in.

For a while Raymond watched her wiping away the tears. 'That's what it'll be like, Jan,' he pointed out gently, 'for all your married life. For your own sake be realistic—do you honestly think the love you say you have for him will stand up to his inability to resist the lure of other women?'

Was Rik really as weak as Raymond seemed to believe? How could a father know a son's strengths, she reasoned, as well as that son's lover knew them? To her, Rik was like the 'steel' of his name; it was part of the reason why her arms, mind and love reached out to him. And why her heart ached for him.

'There's no harm in hoping, is there?' she answered with a shaky smile. 'It's said to spring eternal. Didn't you know?'

CHAPTER NINE

Two days later, Raymond left to visit his old friend Celia Lacey. He shook hands with his son, holding Rik's shoulder.

'You're working too hard, Richard,' he said, glancing at his son's face. 'No play is bad for a man. I'm beginning to regret I piled all Steele Construction's troubles on to your plate.' He turned to Jan, kissing her warmly on both cheeks. 'Over to you now, my dear. He's yours to talk sense into.'

No, he isn't mine! she cried silently, but said aloud, 'To soothe his savage breast, you mean?' Her smile was wide and must have looked genuine, because Raymond seemed relieved. He nodded.

'Whatever it is a fiancée does for her husband-to-be these days. Modern ways . . .' He shook his head. 'I can't even pretend to understand them.'

To Jan, those two days had seemed never-ending. The nights had been long and empty, with only the sound of Rik's voice talking on the telephone to tell her he was there. During the day they had scarcely met, and when they had Rik had been on his way out of the door and she had been passing through to the kitchen to cook meals for Raymond and herself.

That evening, she and Rik would be alone in the house for the first time since Raymond's arrival. Jan's heart thumped at the prospect. But Rik didn't even appear for the evening meal which Jan was looking forward to sharing with him.

'Tied up,' he'd explained briefly by telephone. A husky laugh in the background told Jan to whom he was 'tied'.

Nothing held Jan's attention, not even the new comedy show on television. Part of her fretted, the other part told her not to be so naïve. No man worked flat out, as Rik had been doing, without a break of some kind—preferably, a break shared with an attractive woman. Pictures arose in Jan's mind of Rik and Nadia dining, Rik and Nadia dancing, Rik and Nadia . . .

She squeezed her eyes shut and covered her ears. She must stop tormenting herself, stop listening for non-existent footsteps, although even in bed she lay awake, hoping to hear him come in.

Awakening with a jolt, she peered at her watch. Two o'clock, yet Rik still wasn't home? Now she really did expect the worst. The lights she had hopefully left on for him still burned, so she swung from the bed and pulled a wrap around her, seizing a torch for any emergency.

One by one she switched off the lights, hovering outside Rik's office, puzzled by the glow around the door. Her heart began to thud again, but this time with a very real fear.

The door made no sound as she pushed it gently, her eyes large as they peered into the room. On Rik's desk a lamp shed its light over the usual bric-à-brac of paperwork left for next time. Staring round, her heart almost stopped at the sight of the figure, legs extended, head to one side, fast asleep in the one armchair the room contained.

His body seemed all angles and she looked around for something like a footstool on which to rest his feet. A cardboard box was half hidden under a table behind him. Holding her breath, she eased alongside his recumbent body; as she did so, her wrap shifted a folder that rested precariously on a chair. Moving quickly, she broke its fall, pushing it back into place.

He stirred, but seemed to settle back again. Hoisting the box to the other end of him, she lifted his feet on to it. They were bare, his shoes having been kicked aside. He was jacketless, his partly unbuttoned shirt revealing an area of dark fuzz which her fingers itched to explore.

Tearing her eyes from his lean, totally relaxed form, she started to creep away, but his hand shot out, capturing her wrist. Suddenly she was sprawling in an undignified manner on top of him.

'Rik!' she shrieked. 'You gave me a fright. You weren't asleep, after all.'

'I was,' he growled, 'until a baby elephant tiptoed into the room, creating chaos with a swing of its trunk.'

Jan struggled to free herself from his wrap-around hold, only to find it tightening as if he were clinging to an upturned boat in stormy seas.

'Just let me go,' she exclaimed, 'then you can turn back into the Sleeping Beauty, with——' she rubbed the back of her hand against his jaw, 'with stubble. All I wanted to do was to make you comfortable.'

'Oh, I'm very comfortable, thanks,' he murmured, lips against her hair. 'In fact, I feel as though I'm lying on a cloud with Venus in my arms. What man could ask for more?'

Firm fingers tilted her face and a kiss took charge of her mouth. When the coolly demanding lips paused in their seductive caress, she managed to gasp, 'I only came down to turn out the lights. I thought you weren't home yet. I thought you'd decided to spend the night with——' She chopped off the name. Much more and he'd be accusing her of jealousy.

'Well, you were wrong. At the moment, there's only one woman I want to spend the night with, and by sheer coincidence, she threw herself into my arms. Did you know you were walking into my dream?'

Jan shook her head, peering into his grey eyes and seeing laughter lurking. His hand roamed, finding an entrance through the stretch-neckline of her nightdress, trailing her skin and cradling a softly yielding breast.

Her breath caught in her throat, her body tingling and shifting on his. There was an immediate response beneath her, and she trembled, moistening her lips. If he wanted her as much as she wanted him . . . Her hand went walkabout, discovering the mat of hair she had earlier longed to touch, her fingers indulging themselves now, scraping and tugging in the dark, fuzzy jungle.

Rik shifted her so that his lips could take over the tormenting play of his hand, sucking and nipping, until her head fell back and she burned with desire, crying out with pleasure.

Easing her upright, he rose, fitting his arms around her now totally pliant form. 'Bed,' he murmured huskily. 'I think that's what you're saying?'

His eyes mocked and she shook her head indignantly. '*You* said it to me,' she retorted.

'You've been saying it with every look and action,' he averred mockingly. 'Be honest and admit that I've merely put your thoughts into words.'

She struggled again, but he would not have it, swinging her up the stairs and into her room, closing the door emphatically with a broad, muscled shoulder.

*   *   *

Next morning, Jan stretched, revelling in the ease of her limbs, the sweet contentment of her mind, and wished that she was not alone. Memories of the night swamped her thoughts, turning into half-dreams as she recalled Rik's lovemaking, the demands he had made, his responses to her impudent provocation.

Descending the stairs, refreshed from her shower and cool in her cotton trousers and white short-sleeved shirt, she listened for Rik's voice, but the house was empty of his presence—except that it lingered in every shadowy corner.

There was a note on the kitchen table. 'Gone to a meeting in London,' it said. 'Time of return unknown. Will call you if I have to stay in town. Rik.'

No greeting, no warmth, just businesslike and to the point. Like their marriage deal. Angrily, Jan crushed the piece of paper and threw it down. Except that they weren't married yet. I won't let him near me, she vowed, nor even touch me again until the wedding's over. How could I have been so stupid as to have let him have so much so soon? But if you hadn't, a small voice reminded her, it would have been Nadia's arms he would have gone to instead . . .

Late that afternoon, a ring at the doorbell, followed by a thump, startled her into action. Rik had come home, and in a bad mood?

'Hi,' said Tony joylessly, 'is Big Bad Boss around?'

'He's in London. Why?' Jan asked curiously. 'Did you want to beg for your job back?'

'What do you take me for?' Tony answered, putting a foot in the door. 'A member of the canine species?'

Jan's head said 'come on in'. 'You do look a bit like a bullied puppy. Your tail's down and your ears are flopping.'

'Bow-wow,' said Tony. 'Thanks a lot!'

Jan closed the door and led the way into the living-room.

'Do you think he'd give me my job back if I asked him nicely? Or,' his eyes came to life momentarily, 'if *you* did?'

'I couldn't do that, Tony,' she said gently. 'Outside my sphere. I'm sorry.'

'I did introduce you to him—in a sense, didn't I? After all, I helped you gatecrash his party. In a roundabout way, I've provided him with a wife.'

'In a roundabout way,' Jan echoed a little doubtfully.

Tony threw himself into a chair, glancing at the ornamental clock on the mantelpiece. 'Everything stops for tea,' he said, an eyebrow cocked, hope in his smile.

Jan laughed. 'Hint taken. With or without milk and sugar?'

'With the first, without the second. You know, golden girl,' he shouted after her, 'considering how *friendly* we are, there's a hell of a lot you don't know about me.'

'Well,' Jan called over the noise of the kettle coming to the boil, 'there's a lot I do know. Like—you've got a nice personality, quick with the sympathy.' She appeared with a tea tray. 'Pleasant face, brown eyes, with plenty of latent—er—masculine vigour.'

'For heaven's sake, love, you make it like I'm in a beauty contest! Hey', he did a double-take, 'what d'you mean—*latent*?'

Jan laughed at his outrage. 'Well'—how could she soothe his male pride?—'it's all there, Tony, when you——' She cleared her throat.

'Go on, say it, "when I grow up".'

He dragged a packet of cigarettes from his jacket pocket. Don't, Jan was about to plead, then she drew back, remembering the pride she'd failed to soothe. By the time Rik got home, the smell would have dispersed, especially if she opened all the windows when Tony had gone . . .

'Try for me,' he appealed on the doorstep, 'I need that job, Jan, honest I do. I give my mum some cash each week to help her. Except that I can't now, can I?'

Jan was deeply moved, remembering her efforts to help her own parents. 'I won't make any promises,' she sighed, 'but——'

'That's my doorstep baby,' he said, hugging her and swinging her round.

It was almost bedtime when the key turned in the front door. Her yawn turned into a gasp. Thank goodness she'd taken the precaution of clearing the air when Tony had gone!

'Hi, Rik.' Her smile was wide, her heart racing. 'I've missed you, darling. The day's seemed so long.'

Door held open with his foot, he waved into the darkness. A horn honked, wheels spun on gravel and tore away. I'd know that horn anywhere, Jan thought, her heart sinking.

Pivoting, she made for the living-room, confronting him. 'London, you told me in your note. Had a meeting, you said, time of return unknown. Why weren't you honest?' she stormed. 'Why didn't you tell me where you were really going? Why didn't your note say, "Spending the day with Nadia, her arms are more experienced than yours"?'

'How biased can you get in your judgement of another woman?' Rik responded, carelessly flinging down his jacket which had been draped over his arm.

His words hurt like the twist of a knife. 'So Nadia's like Caesar's wife, above suspicion, beyond reproach?'

'She's a partner in the firm of accountants I deal with,' he shot at her. 'She's a financial adviser—*my* financial adviser. Now have I silenced your crazy accusations?'

A sob shook Jan's throat. She swallowed it and whispered, 'I'm sorry.' He gazed at her, expression enigmatic. 'It's just that . . . well, she may be clever, but she's a woman too, and——'

He dropped his briefcase and took her in his arms, rubbing his cheek against her hair. 'And my God, you're a woman, Janetta, all woman——' Unaccountably, Jan felt him stiffen.

'I didn't know you smoked.' His tone was questioning, yet dangerous.

She frowned. 'You know I don't.' Then, on a little gasp, 'I——' It was no use, he'd caught her out.

'The day's been a long one, has it? So who's the secret lover who made it go faster?'

She was so sure she'd cleared the air of smoke. Following his eyes, she saw what he had seen. Cigarette stubs, seven or eight of them . . . she'd clean forgotten to empty the ashtray her visitor had used.

'Tony's not——' Hastily, Jan checked herself. She had given him away! How could she plead now on his behalf? 'He called in, that's all.' She disengaged herself from his arms, feeling guilty although she was entirely innocent. 'It's his job—he wants it back, Rik.'

'He does? And he thought he'd achieve his aim by making up to my fiancée in my absence?'

She'd blown it, she had to admit, but still she pleaded, 'He helps his mother every week with money.'

'You mean you fell for that heartstring-plucker?'

Jan's heart sank at Rik's sardonic response to Tony's claim that his mother depended on him financially. Wasn't she in a similar situation? Hadn't she accepted his father's highly remunerative job to offer to help *her* parents? When she finally told him, would he react with the same cynical disbelief?

'Moore wants it for drink, nothing else,' Rik dismissed. 'It's not the first time his work's suffered as a result of his absenteeism. Take him back? Not on your life! He's a lazy, feckless idler——'

'No, he's not!' Jan cried unguardedly. 'He's good-natured, open and warm——'

The grey eyes had darkened, lit by storm warnings. 'So that's how the land lies,' he snarled. 'Let me make it quite clear, Janetta. If you run into his arms, you'll run right out of our marriage deal and all the goodies from your point of view that it carries with it.'

She didn't want Tony, but the injustice of what Rik was saying hit her squarely. 'If you can have an extra-marital female in your life, and you know who I mean,' she declared heatedly, if a little unwisely, 'I can have an extra-marital male friend if I want!'

'Oh, no,' said Rik said through tight lips, 'that wasn't part of the *job* contract we agreed between us, and you know it. Will you excuse me?' he added icily. 'I've got an appointment with a shower. Then

I'm getting down to some work.' At the door, he paused. 'The next time you entertain a male in my absence, if you want to become Mrs Rik Steele and live in luxury for the rest of your life, you'd better take care to remove the evidence before I get home.'

Rik seemed to spend half the night working. Now and then, Jan heard the ring of the telephone.

'Tokyo?' she heard him ask briskly on one occasion, his voice carrying in the empty silence. 'Steele Construction here, head office. I wish to speak to——' A long conversation had followed and the English language had seemed to be interspersed with a foreign tongue; which could only mean, Jan surmised, that Rik knew some words of Japanese.

'Los Angeles?' he queried half an hour later. 'I wish to speak to Ted Hannaway. He's the guy in charge there, isn't he? Rik Steele here, Steele Construction, head office, London, England. Yes, yes,' with slight impatience, 'R Steele junior.'

Except, Jan thought, pulling the pillow around her head, there's nothing *junior* about that man! And this house is a good few miles from London . . .

After that, he seemed to be talking at length to Buenos Aires and heaven knew where else in the world. Fretfully, Jan tossed and turned. It wasn't his voice that disturbed her, so much as his presence in the house. Not to mention, and she blushed at the thought, the absence of him from her bed.

Thoughts tumbled around her brain . . . If Rik decried Tony's claim of helping his mother financially, how would he take her own claim of accepting his money and offer of marriage in order to help her parents? With the same deep cynicism, she suspected. Try telling him, part of her cried, just try.

But she closed her mind to the thought.

Walking sleepily down the stairs, she heard him say, 'Right. The day after tomorrow, then. Yes, we'll come to a meal, Mrs Hart. I won't disturb Janetta—I'm sure she'll agree. I'm looking forward to meeting you, too.'

As the receiver clattered down, Jan swung inward with the door. 'I'm here, I'm awake. Why didn't you tell me my mother had called?' Her hand reached for the telephone. 'I'll ring her now.'

His fingers clamped around her wrist. 'Oh, no. I've heard about never-ending mother-and-daughter conversations. I'm waiting for an international call. I want the lines clear.'

'But——' She *had* to speak to her mother, to put her in the picture about her true relationship with Rik. On the other hand, she couldn't, could she? 'You're being honest with me?' her mother had asked on hearing the news. 'You love this man you've chosen?' 'Madly,' she'd answered, with total honesty.

Jan gestured helplessly. 'If it's all settled——'

'It is.'

Looming over her, shirt open and hanging free, he stirred primitive longings inside her that overwhelmed her at that time of the morning. It was bad enough that she'd spent the night fighting her instincts to run to him . . .

It was clear that his thoughts had been anywhere but with her. Bristly jaw shadow competed with the darkness around his eyes, telling of a night of international commerce over the telephone wires and precious little, if any, sleep.

It wasn't until they were drinking tea in Rik's office mid-afternoon that Jan ventured to raise the subject. He had shaved and showered, and these acts alone seemed to have renewed his vigour. All day she had been helping him, forcing herself to switch off whenever he was near, taking a hold on her feelings when sometimes he pressed against her shoulder to check a letter she was holding.

It had been a strain acting the perfect secretary, filing papers and documents, all the while experiencing the tension of the proximity, yet having to pretend her mind was on the business in hand.

What were his feelings? she wondered. Strictly business too? Once, when he'd leant over to read a paragraph of a document she was typing, she thought she had heard his soft intake of breath in the region of her newly shampooed hair. Then she had told herself severely that it was wishful thinking on her part and that she really should keep her mind on her work.

'Rik?' She swallowed some tea. 'About our visit to my parents tomorrow evening.'

He was half seated on the desk, cup half-way to his lips, the other hand negligently in his pocket. Jan's eyes met his and she saw that the shadows around them persisted. She marvelled at his stamina. All day he had not taken a single moment's rest, yet she was certain he had worked through the night.

'Hm?' he asked, looking at her over the rim of the cup. 'What's wrong? Is there some dark secret you're harbouring about them?'

Jan blushed deeply, then cursed her own involuntary reaction. He was too near the truth for comfort. 'Of course not!' She hoped she sounded convincingly indignant. 'It's just . . . well,' she swilled the contents in her cup and drank for time to think, 'they—they think we're deeply in love.'

'And?'

Was he being deliberately obtuse? 'Well, I—I should hate to disillusion them. Especially my mother. She's so pleased about us. She——' her eyes swung away, then back, '—she reads romantic novels.'

Rik smiled, comprehending. 'So that's where her daughter gets her yen for romance from? And for your mother's benefit you want me to pretend to be in love with you and behave like a romantic hero?'

Jan pushed her cup away. 'Well, if you—if you wouldn't mind?' His chuckle encouraged her. 'What I mean is——'

'I know what you mean. It won't be at all difficult. In fact,' he added softly, 'it'll be my pleasure. This, for instance?' His cup met its saucer and he swung her chair so that she faced him. Hauling her into his arms, he kissed her until she begged for mercy and her lips ached from the onslaught of his.

As he looked deep into her eyes, his expression changed. 'She's willing. Good grief, all day I must have been blind.' He swung her towards the door, then the phone rang and he cursed roundly.

Seated at his desk, he took the call, and Jan knew he was lost to her. Somewhere in the southern hemisphere, she gathered. Thousands of miles away . . .

All next day Jan worked with Rik. In the night, she had heard him tread the stairs with heavy steps. Her watch told her it was the early hours, yet he had hardly seemed to have retired to rest when the telephone split the silence again. It was barely dawn for them, yet in other places in the world the working day was proceeding at a fast pace.

By the time the overseas conversations had finished—Rik seemed to have answered from his bedroom—he had plainly decided that it way useless to try to get back to sleep. Jan had heard him rise and shower and go downstairs.

Now, at the afternoon's end, his eyes looked heavy again, yet his manner was as brisk and keen as ever. Again she wondered at his energy which, deprived of sleep though he was, seemed unabated.

'If you want to postpone our visit, Rik——' she began, but he cut in,

'To my prospective parents-in-law? Not on your life! I've been looking forward to it.'

Jan's heart jumped, then raced. His mood was good. For hours they had worked well together. 'I'm pleased with you, Janetta,' he'd said only half an hour ago. 'You give good value for money.' His eyes had narrowed. 'In more ways than one.'

'Thanks a lot,' she answered, pretending nonchalance, but her heart had leapt at the compliment, double-sided though it was.

In the car, Rik's good mood had persisted.

Moistening her lips, she ventured, 'If I—if I told you, Rik, that I accepted your money and your marriage offer for the sake of my parents, would you believe me?'

He frowned, his profile hard. 'I don't get you.'

'To—to help them financially, because they're short of cash——'

His laugh was short and sardonic. Her heart dived. She should have known.

'With a mother who owns an expensive fur wrap and parents who were wealthy enough to give you a gold chain—and a good one at that—for your twenty-first?' His hand patted hers. 'Pull the other one, Miss Hart.'

'Heartstring-plucker, you called it when Tony Moore made the same claim,' Jan retorted, telling herself she should have known better than to hope he might believe her. 'I suppose you're dismissing my statement in the same cynical terms?'

He seemed to be concentrating on his driving.

'Give me one good reason,' she persisted, 'why I shouldn't be telling you the truth about my parents needing my help.'

There was the merest pause. 'We'll wait and see, shall we?'

And you will see, Jan thought, her heart leaping in anticipation of his humble apology for not believing her, *only a few minutes from now*. When he saw her parents' plight he would forgive her utterly and take back all the accusations he had flung at her of acquisitiveness and gold-digging.

Her mother's arms engulfed her on the doorstep, her father's smiling face lighting up the background. Jan had not seen them so happy for years. There was a paternal handshake for Rik, admiration in bright maternal eyes as Penelope shyly reached up to kiss her future son-in-law's cheek.

In the sitting-room a silver salver groaned under the weight of half a dozen bottles, crystal glasses glinted in the glow of newly-fitted wall lights. A new and costly carpet covered the floor, while expensive furniture that Jan had never seen arranged itself welcomingly in the seating area.

Heart plummeting, Jan felt her hand grow moist within the clasp of Rik's beside her. How could she ever expect him to believe now that she had been speaking the truth about her parents' need for her financial help?

Disentangling her hand—Rik, deep in conversation with her father, did not seem to notice—she followed her mother into the kitchen, and found a fresh shock awaiting her. Shining new kitchen equipment greeted her eyes—refrigerator, deep-freeze, washing machine—all of them new and brightly gleaming. The brand names they bore told the world that they were the best in their particular line, and, of course, the most expensive.

'Mother,' Jan got out, 'however did you——'

'Manage to buy all this when we haven't a penny to our name?' Penelope laughed, and it was a happy, carefree sound. 'I have to admit it—we borrowed from the bank, in advance of your marriage to Rik. Would you believe Mr Fuller, our bank manager, knows all about your young man. Richard Steele owns a fine company, he told us. He said it's called Dancing River.'

Jan nodded. 'But I'm——' Not married to him yet, she had been about to say, but her mother broke in,

'We told him you were going to marry Rik, and he was going to be our son-in-law. And lo and behold,' she made as if to wave a wand, 'all our broken-down fixtures and fittings vanished and all this wonderful new stuff took its place. Just like a fairy-tale! Mr Fuller said how romantic it all was. Oh, Jan darling,' Penelope hugged her daughter, 'I'm so happy for you! It's obvious from the way Rik looks at you that he's head over heels. And, darling, he's so handsome!'

What if I told her the truth? Jan wondered helplessly. What if I said he doesn't really love me, he's only pretending? Because he thinks I want that money for myself? But she knew she could never bring herself to tread on all her mother's dreams of happiness ever after.

'Mum,' she found herself whispering, 'now Rik's going to be one of the family, do I have your and Dad's permission to tell him——'

'About us? About your father losing his job?' Penelope looked aghast. 'Oh no, dear, I'm quite sure Edward wouldn't want Rik to know. Especially in view of Rik's high position—well, he is important in the business world, isn't he? And very well off. We——' she patted Jan's head and scurried on with her work, 'we have our pride, Jan dear, especially your father. We're telling Rik Edward's taken early retirement.'

Early retirement? Jan thought. At barely fifty years old? In Rik's cold reasoning eyes, that could only point to a bank account so brimming that there was no financial necessity for her father ever to work again. After the statement she had made on their way there, whereabouts in his estimation would that leave her?

Above the chinking of crystal and bone china—all new to Jan's eyes—she heard her own heart breaking. Their pride! she thought, swallowing a lump in her throat. What about my fiancé's opinion of me, of my integrity? Wasn't that just as important? But she knew she could never tell her parents about the true situation between Rik and herself. Her mother—romantic as she was—would never believe it, anyway.

'Where's that woman of mine?' Rik was at the kitchen door, his eagle glance sweeping round and coming to rest on his fiancée. Only she could read his message—hard-up parents, you said, needing your money to help them keep their heads high, not to say above water? Pull the other one, I told you, didn't

I? And how right I was!

He pounced and his arm went round her. On the surface, Rik was playing the part of doting lover to perfection. With a delighted chuckle, Penelope busied herself with her preparations for the meal.

Rik pulled his fiancée into the entrance hall, his lips nuzzled her ear. 'Little liar, my love,' she heard him whisper. 'What did you take me for, an idiot? But I knew what you were from the start, my mercenary messenger. The girl with not just one itching palm but two.'

Jan made to swing away, but her mother bustled through at that moment, so escape from Rik's iron hold was impossible. 'You——' she started to whisper, but his mouth descended, cutting off her angry riposte.

As they were driving home the silence between them boded ill for her, she was sure of it. To break it, she switched on a tape. Her mother had admired her ring, her father wanted to know what date they had in mind for the wedding ceremony, so that he and her mother could make a list of guests, arrange the wedding breakfast and book a hall . . . with all the confidence of a man with half a fortune to lavish on the marriage of his only daughter. Jan had squirmed inside, not daring to raise her eyes and look into Rik's, knowing she would see only castigation and scorn in them.

The taped music filling the car was romantic and seemed to set Rik's teeth on edge. The movement of a furious hand stopped the tape in its tracks.

Standing back, stiffly polite, to allow her to enter the house, he passed her on his way to the drinks cabinet in the living-room.

'Rik?' No answer. He tossed the liquid down his

throat, his back to her. 'I—I could explain.'

'So, explain. I'm a captive audience.'

His arctic tones turned her blood to ice. She couldn't, could she, not without betraying her parents' trust?

'Have no fear, Janetta,' Rik grated, 'my views of your character have merely been confirmed. I've no intention of going back on our marriage deal. You will still become my wife.' He swung round, eyes burning. 'You need the money and the wordly goods my financial status can give you, so I know for certain that *you* won't back out.'

Lifting her shoulders, Jan made her way to her room, sinking to the bed and lying back lifelessly.

He must be tireless, she thought a couple of hours later, listening to him talking on the telephone again. She had not slept either, turning and tossing, her throat tight with holding back the tears. What use would it be to let them come? She was caught in a trap and there was no one to hear her cries for help.

She must have drifted into sleep, because she stirred to find an arm across her breast, another beneath her, and the deep breathing of an exhausted man. In his state of deep fatigue he had come to her! Her heart did a dance, but collapsed in a heap when cold reason told her that exhaustion must have caused Rik to lose his way and enter her room instead of his own.

Later in the night, a voice grazed her ear. 'Mercenary woman though you are,' it was saying, 'I can't resist you. Your body's like a magnet to mine . . .'

He turned her, tugging her nightdress over her head and running his hands all over her, stroking and arousing her in all her secret places in the way he knew would give her pleasure. He shifted on to her, taking her mouth over in a deeply passionate kiss, thrusting into her until tears of ecstasy filled her eyes, and her lips and tongue combined to gasp his name as he took her with him to the summit.

CHAPTER TEN

'I SHALL be away for two or three days,' the note propped on the breakfast-table told Jan. 'I've called a meeting in London of Steele Construction's board of directors. If you feel inclined, there are a couple of reports on the computer I'd be glad to have printed out. Thanks in advance. Rik.'

No words of love, Jan thought, no softening of the memo's businesslike tone because she was so special, much more to him than a mere clerical assistant.

She sighed, then reproached herself for sleeping on until almost midday. If she hadn't been so tired, if she hadn't been so fulfilled with Rik's love-making . . . At least she would have had his parting kiss to hug to her in his absence.

Or would she? In Rik's office, there was the faintest lingering trace of perfume. I don't need three guesses, Jan thought, to identify its wearer. In an ashtray were three cigarette stubs. If she hadn't already guessed, the lipstick stains on the stubs would have confirmed Nadia's recent presence. Snap! she thought miserably. Who hasn't cleared away the evidence now?

Suppressing her anger, she drank coffee and printed out the reports Rik had referred to. She worked automatically, her thoughts tearing her apart. He had risen from her bed, warm from her arms, and gone straight into Nadia's.

Putting the sheets of the document together, Jan

wondered how much longer she could take Rik's divided loyalties in her stride. But how could she walk out on Rik now, when her parents had spent in advance the money she had promised them—Rik's money?

All the same, she had somehow to find a way of hardening herself to Rik's continuing devotion to the woman he really loved, married though she still was to another man.

To intensify her unhappiness, the weather had turned grey, cloud finally ousting the sun from the sky. For nearly twenty-four hours it rained ceaselessly, the darkened sky lowering her spirits unbearably. In the empty silence of the night, she sobbed her heart out, falling at last into an exhausted sleep.

Next morning the sun reappeared, but it found her no nearer to accepting Rik's unswerving devotion to Nadia. It came to her suddenly—she would have to get away so that she could think . . .

Throwing a few personal belongings into a case, she made her way to the Merry Maid's Arms. At reception, where she booked in for a couple of days, there was no sign of Don Heeley, the landlord of the inn and Rik's friend. He might—just—have asked questions, to which there would be no answers.

On Rik's desk she had left a note: 'I'm sorry,' she had written, 'but I can't go on like this. Your lack of trust in me is slowly poisoning me—my feelings, my thoughts, my life. Forgive me for sounding so melodramatic, as I'm sure you'll call it, but all of it is true. I've gone away to think. Janetta.'

Seated that afternoon among the fragrant blooms around the inn's patio bordering the river, she swallowed her tears and wondered how she was going to cope with the rest of her life as Rik's unloved wife.

A shout brought her out of her unhappy reverie. 'Hi there, doorstep baby! What're you doing there? Drowning your sorrows? Or have you left the boss high and dry?'

'Mapping out the rest of my life,' she answered with candour, although Tony did not believe it.

He laughed. 'You must be joking. You're marrying the boss, aren't you? He's the one who'll do the mapping—for both of you. He'll plan the route—all the way to journey's end. And you'll be the one who tags along behind. Mark my words, golden girl. I know Rik Steele better than you.' He made a face. 'Hey, have you tackled him about my job?'

'I'm choosing my moment,' she answered. 'His mood's got to be right, you should know that.'

Tony was bobbing about in a small blue and white cabin cruiser, hanging on to the hotel's private mooring platform. 'Come and join us,' he sang, 'Oh, come on, Jan. I could do with a bit of company.'

The pleading note brought her to the river's edge.

'What do you think of her?' asked Tony, pride in his voice. 'I found her in Steele & Mountford's junk yard. Mick Mountford said I could have it for free, but I'd have to put in a lot of work. So I did, and I got her going. Look, I've kept her name—*Riverjoy*.' He thrust out a hand. 'Come for a ride.'

'Sure it's river-worthy?' Jan asked doubtfully.

'She's watertight and skims like a bird through the waves,' he assured her poetically. Her hesitation persisted and his face dropped. 'Keep me company, Jan. Being out of work when you've always had a pocketful of cash is the other side of hell. And having to keep on disappointing my mum . . . know how it is?'

Indeed she did, most certainly she knew. Gingerly she stepped down, gripping the helping hand and steadying herself.

'Right,' exclaimed Tony joyfully. 'Let's go!'

The motor roared, the boat half lifted, then leapt forward, unbalancing Jan so that she dropped on to a hard bench seat near to Tony. He piloted the boat well, Jan noticed, pleasantly surprised at his competence.

'I didn't know you had it in you,' she joked above the noise of the motor.

'You'd be surprised!' he shouted back, pleased by her praise. 'Before I got to work on this baby, she was a heap of junk. Look at her now, lovely clean lines, cuts through the water. Jumping for joy, isn't she? Living up to her name.'

The riverbanks sped past, walkers on the towpath looked on with admiring eyes as *Riverjoy's* fresh new paintwork gleamed in the sun. On a shelf in the cabin, Jan noticed the inevitable unopened cans, but when Tony reached inside for a couple of them, offering her one, she was glad to see that they were non-alcoholic. Perhaps Rik's dismissal had taught him a lesson, after all?

'Hey there, Tony,' a man's voice hailed from the towpath, 'what do you think you're doing, hijacking your boss's lady?' His dog barked and raced on.

It was Don Heeley, landlord of the Merry Maid's Arms. He had recognised her, Jan realised with dismay, even from that distance. When he saw her name in the hotel's register, would he betray her hiding-place to Rik?

'This shipmate's a friend of mine,' Tony shouted back, putting his arm around her. 'Close friend,' he added cheekily, proposing 'toast' with his upraised, bubbling can.

'Ho, ho,' the landlord called, plainly scenting a non-existent intrigue. His dog barked again and scuffled impatiently and the man followed, whistling, 'What shall we do with a drunken sailor?'

Like background music with a threat interwoven into its theme came the persistent roar of the weir. It wasn't yet in sight, and Jan relaxed. Tony would know when to turn back. The Thames was his playground. This venture with *Riverjoy* was simply an extension of his hobby.

'Not distracting the boss today, then?' Tony asked over the engine's throb.

'He's away for a couple of days.'

'So while the cat's away, Jan will play? Which is how you found the courage to come with me,' Tony joked. 'I'd better deliver you back safe and sound, otherwise he might—hey, what the . . .?'

The current changed its mood, playing with them dangerously, buffeting them and swinging them sideways. They must have intruded on the fringes of the wash from the weir. As they had rounded a bend, it swung into view, its magnetic power reaching out even beyond what appeared to be its limits.

Overlooking it was the Rushing River hotel where, Jan remembered, Rik had wined and dined her that wonderful evening. People were seated on the terrace, drinking afternoon tea beneath colourful umbrellas.

'What the hell——' Tony swore over the sound of the spluttering motor. It seemed to be angry that he was expecting so much of it in the circumstances. He could not seem to guide the tiny cruiser in the direction he wanted. The unrelenting rain of the previous day had caused the level to rise and the river had swollen considerably, the current unduly strong. The weir swept in a foaming semicircle, wider and louder than Jan remembered. At close quarters it was terrifying, spreading in a great remorseless plunging line across the width of the river.

Gazing at its angry turbulence made Jan feel insignificant and as helpless as a twig caught in its force. With deepending anxiety, she watched Tony's frantic efforts to win the battle.

Striding out from the opposite bank, an extensive walkway spanned the downward rush of white foam, while, at regular intervals across the water, posts defined the outskirts of the weir. In large scarlet letters the word 'Danger' shouted a warning from a white board.

Tony cursed and struggled, straining with all his strength to steer a course away from the whirlpool, but the current swept them inexorably on, nearer and nearer to its menacing roar.

Jan stifled a scream, telling herself that panicking now would help no one.

'Feel like swimming for it?' shouted Tony, half joking, half afraid. 'I'm not sure I can——'

'But, Tony, I'm a poor swimmer!' Jan shrieked, racked with a terrible mounting fear. 'Don't you remember?'

'I certainly do,' Tony answered, 'you got a ducking the first day I met you—oh, for God's sake, no!'

The pull of the weir had trapped them at last and the boat spun and floundered uncontrollably. The hull juddered against a marker post, but the boat, incredibly, remained upright, before beaching itself, as if to gain a breathing space, on the series of wide, semicircular steps over which the great volume of water poured.

'God, Jan, I'm sorry, I'm sorry!' Tony yelled, then the boat fell sideways, tipping them out. 'My boat—oh, my beautiful *Riverjoy*!' Tony moaned as he went under.

Jan found her feet were on the steps and she was upright, but not for long. Her feet were jerked from under her and she was pulled and dragged and pounded by the onrush of the relentless flow.

'Tony!' she screamed. 'Oh, Tony, where are you? I——'

'I'm OK,' came his voice from far away, 'I'm holding on, Jan, try to stay upright——'

But she couldn't. She was being swept along with the foaming water, going under, bouncing up again, blinded and deafened, her breath stolen completely away. Head surfacing, she gasped, mouth wide, greedily sucking in air, but even then it wasn't enough to satisfy her lungs.

Before she died, she wanted so much to tell Rik she loved him. Just once would do . . . Oh, just give me that chance, she begged, then I'll accept whatever's coming . . .

There seemed to be shouts and screams from all directions, then she struck concrete and fell, face down, hitting her forehead, her arms and legs flailing. She couldn't breathe for water, it was in her eyes, her nose, her mouth . . . The weir was tumbling her, it was sweeping her over its frothing, pounding foam. She was bumping down those steps again, the leaping, swirling river roaring remorselessly on.

Her arm made bruising contact with something strong and upright, a marker post, and her instinct shrieked at her to grasp it, grip it, hold on to it for dear life, no matter how the roaring water might try and tear her from it, washing her away for ever.

'She's there, I can see her, but be quick!' Tony's excited shout registered faintly on her exhausted brain. 'I think she's almost flaked out!'

'My God!' a man's voice was gasping. 'Jan, Jan-ett-a . . .'

Strong arms twined around her, tugging her free of the support she had been clinging to, easing her alongside the walkway and swimming with one arm around her to clamber to the side of a familiar, noisy boat, half flooded but righted, and hauling her into it.

'Tony?' It was an anxious whisper, and it came from her own stiff, dry lips. She had lost consciousness, but now she had surfaced again. 'He didn't drown?'

'He's OK,' was the clipped reply.

'It wasn't his fault, Rik. It was——' In vain she tried to recall whose fault it was, but weakness overtook her and she moved her throbbing head helplessly against the softly yielding pillow.

I'm still alive, she thought, rallying a little. I've been given that chance I longed for to tell Rik I love him. What was wrong with telling him now? 'Rik, I——'

'You want something?' He had come to stand beside the bed.

It was the edge to his voice that stopped her. He didn't want to know, did he? He just wasn't interested because her name wasn't Nadia. And because theirs was a business arrangement, with passion in plenty but not a grain of love in sight.

'Nothing, thank you,' she answered tonelessly, and Rik moved away from the bed.

He had carried into her own room. At once the memories came crowding in, of that other time he had pulled her from the river.

'This,' she said, speaking with difficulty because her throat still seemed to be choked with water, although her lips were parched, 'is where we came in.' She tried a smile, but it was painful and fleeting. 'Second time round, you've saved me from drowning.'

I want to drown again . . . in your arms. The thought came unbidden, making tears spring because of the utter impossibility of her ever finding herself in them again.

'Thank you, Rik, for saving my life,' she whispered, saddened by his detachment and cold eyes. 'You must have risked yours in coming to my rescue.'

'The river's in my blood,' he dismissed. 'I've learned to cope with all its moods. But I must admit, I've never had to fight the weir before.'

'How did you know where to find me?

'First thing I did when I'd read your note was to ring the Merry Maid's Arms. The landlord——'

'Don Heeley.' Jan nodded. 'He saw Tony and me on the river.'

'Right. Going downstream. I knew Moore's little weakness——'

'He hadn't drunk a drop!'

'Don said he'd held up a can. To me, that meant only one thing, alcoholic beverage. In other words, beer—cans of it.'

'They weren't alcoholic, Rik. I can vouch for that, because I had some too.'

'All the same, I remembered his drunken state when I fired him. I also knew the weir wasn't that far from where Don had spotted you.'

'So you made a dash.'

'Faster than the speed of sound. The rest, as the saying goes, is history. If——' Rik looked at her intently, 'if the result had been anything but what it was, Moore would have been in orbit by now, sent hurtling—by me—into the limits of outer space.'

In the drive outside, a car drew to a stop. Nadia? Jan wondered tensely. But the style of driving hadn't sounded right. Rik answered the door.

There were voices, raised, in argument, defensive on the visitor's part, with seering anger on Rik's.

'But, boss, it wasn't my fault. The old tub had a will of its own. It bucked like a horse when it felt the drag of that perishing weir. I did my best—ask Jan. Hey, up there,' Tony called daringly, 'golden girl, want to talk to me?'

There was a bristling pause, as though the combatants were waiting, claws unsheathed, for Jan's reply.

Feet took the stairs, two at a time. Rik appeared, eyes burning with the heat of the flight. 'Well, what's the answer?'

'Yes, I do. Please,' Jan answered.

'Hi,' said Tony, voice hushed as if in a sickroom, 'how goes it, Jan?' He sat on the bed, taking her hand. 'Oh, God, love, when I saw you clawing the air and your head bobbing helplessly . . . I can't tell you how I felt. If you hadn't survived, I wouldn't have wanted to——'

'Yes, you would.' Jan reached out to put restraining fingers to his mouth. He kissed the tips of them and held her hand. 'You'd have gone on living, come up smiling. I know you by now, Tony.'

Her smile was faint, but it plainly pleased him.

'You're great for a guy's ego, doorstep baby.' His voice cracked just a little. 'I could go a long way with you believing in me . . .'

Slowly, painfully because her bumps and bruises hurt, Jan shook her head, reaching up to stroke his cheek.

'OK, Moore,' Rik appeared in the doorway, 'time's up.'

Tony kissed the palm of Jan's hand. 'Want to see me again, doorstep baby?'

'I don't mind,' she replied. He was bright and cheerful and, she thought, I could do with those things in my life right now.

It was some time before Rik reappeared, carrying a tray laden with tea things.

'How did you guess?' asked Jan, trying to lighten her vice despite Rik's unbending manner. 'I'm so thirsty, Rik. It's ironic, isn't it, after nearly drowning in liquid?' But she had not even scratched the outer shell of his aloofness.

'Don't sit up,' he ordered, and thankfully she sank back.

Seated on the bed and with his arm to support her, he helped her moisten her lips, then sip the hot, reviving liquid. She wanted his arms to enfold her, soothing away all her aches and pains, but his manner was as remote as that of a doctor attending a patient.

Rik left her then, and she slipped into a soothing sleep, wakening again when she became conscious of his presence in the room.

'There's no need to nurse me, Rik,' she told him. 'You must have work to do, your father's affairs as well as your own.'

'You want me to go?'

How should she answer that? she wondered. If she said 'yes', he would take it as a dismissal; if 'no', he would begin to fret about the paperwork that needed attention, phone calls to be made.'

'I——'

The telephone cut into her answer. It might not have been Nadia calling at the house earlier in the day, but it was certainly Nadia calling now, filling his ear with words which seemed to rivet him, commanding every bit of his attention.'

Rik's back was to her and Jan pushed away the bedcovers, pulled the bedroom door shut behind her and crept shakily to the bathroom. Filling the bath, she climbed in quickly, lying back and letting the heated water flow over her bruised body.

'For God's sake, what do you think you're doing?'

Rik burst in, and her eyes flew wide with fright. The water had gone cold, which meant she must have drifted off.

'Of all the mindless things to do!' Rik admonished. 'Good grief,' his hands plunged in and lifted her bodily, standing her down and wrapping the towel around her slender figure, 'as if *two* near-drownings weren't enough, she has to go and put herself in dire danger of a third?'

With exquisite gentleness, he rubbed her all over, but it was as if he were dealing with a child, his expression was so impassive. Which could only mean, Jan thought sadly, that she was no longer attractive to him. Contrarily, despite her weakened state, no matter where he touched her, Jan felt her body responding. She had to grit her teeth to withstand the flood of feeling the movement of his hands was releasing within her.

'So you don't like me touching you,' he remarked

grimly, unwinding the towel, his eyes lingering for a few tormenting seconds on the bruises and grazes showing starkly against the smooth whiteness of her skin. Lips thinning, he eased the nightdress over her head. 'Unfortunately for you, in the circumstances, you'll have to put up with it. Of course,' with deep cynicism, 'if you'd prefer me to call Moore back——'

'You're quite wrong,' Jan cried. 'I don't object to——' your hands on my body, she had almost said. If she had spoken them, he would have taken them to mean that she was intending to force him to hold him to his promise to marry her. 'Tony's a friend, nothing else.'

'You expect me to believe that after the way you've just welcomed him, the way you defend him every time his name crops up?'

'It's only because of the way you're always criticising him. He's got something, Rik, more than you think. *Riverjoy* was a write-off, but he brought it back to life. He repaired it and painted it——'

'*That* was *Riverjoy*? But she was a heap of old junk. We threw her out for scrap.'

'Tony told me. But Mr Mountford told him he could have it for nothing, and you've seen the result. Rik——' her hand stretched out appealingly '—don't take that boat away from him. It's all he's got now he doesn't have a job.'

'What do you take me for?' gritted Rik. 'A heartless swine?'

If he knew what I really thought of him, Jan whispered secretly, how much I admire and love him . . . But that was a story that could never be told.

It was later, after a light meal that Rik had brought her, and she was lying alone, that she made herself face the fact that their marriage now was surely quite out of the question. After all, hadn't she run for cover, as good as deserting him, leaving that note? As sleep began to claim her, the thought slid into her mind, then into her dreams, that their relationship had reached the parting of the ways.

The dream turned into a nightmare. Her heart pounded, the blood in her veins going crazy. She heard shouts, felt water gushing over her head, impelling her along. She couldn't see, she couldn't breathe, she couldn't even cry for help . . . She was drowning again, and this time there was no one to rescue her, pull her back to life and living . . .

Arms enclosed her, stilling her struggling body, forcing her limbs to stop their threshing and kicking, an iron hand around her ankles making them obey the command of the deep and vibrant voice . . .

'Lie still, Janetta, It's all behind you. You're safe in my arms.'

The nightmare began to recede, reason prevailing, but it took a long time for her heart to regain its normal beat. Then a shivering began that she could not control. Turning her overheated flesh towards the hard angles of the man who held her, she reached out, clinging to the sureness and security of his overwhelming strength. Wrapping herself around him, she cried bitter tears, her cheek to his chest.

For hours, it seemed, Rik held her, and even when the crying died away and she became still he did not leave. Slowly, she relaxed in those arms' compelling hold, drifting into dreams so sweet she was certain she would die of happiness.

The man she loved was beside her, kissing her and stroking her, whispering of his love, and of his belief in her for evermore . . .

*   *   *

It was all a dream, of course, because by morning he had gone, with only the imprint of his body to tell her that his presence beside her, at least, had been a reality.

Jan slept again, waking when her instinct told her someone else was in the room.

'I feel better, Rik,' she said, her voice sounding thin and high. 'I want to get up.'

'Stay right where you are,' he commanded, looking down at her, his expression aloof. 'After what you've been through, you need rest.'

'No, I don't, I——' Swinging her legs down, she tested them for strength, but they failed to carry her and she fell forward into Rik's waiting arms. She held her breath, waiting for them to enfold her and pull her close, but his support was utterly impersonal as he led her back to the bed.

'I won't say "I told you so",' he reproved. 'Will you do as you're told for once?'

'I didn't believe you,' she answered with a touch of the old impudence, gazing up at him as she lay against the pillows. 'Now perhaps you know what it feels like.'

His mouth curved slightly and his eyebrows lifted, but, if he had a riposte in mind, it didn't make it to his lips.

All that day he remained within hearing, working in his office, making calls and answering them. At regular intervals he supplied her with hot drinks and food, plumping up her pillows and overseeing every move she made outside of bed.

Even when she took a bath, he was there again, tending her wounds after helping to dry her. He could not know how she burned inside at his every touch, her heart swelling with gratitude for his tenderness, yet throbbing with longing for even the smallest sign of arousal within him through his tactile contact with her body, let alone the sight of her nakedness on his masculine reflexes.

Next morning she was up and dressed before he could remonstrate within her, going unsteadily down the stairs to confront him with her *fait accompli*, but he was missing.

He erupted into the kitchen a few minutes later, fresh from an early morning run, cotton T-shirt adhering to his torso, beads of moisture across his forehead and upper lip. When his breathing had steadied, his hands found his hips.

'Determined little devil, aren't you?' he commented. 'OK, so you've put one over on me. When I've showered, I'll cook something and we'll eat.'

'Please don't bother on my account,' answered Jan, surprised by the firmness in her voice. 'A piece of toast is all I'll——'

'I said,' Rik put in through his teeth, 'we'll eat. And I didn't mean nibble. Get me?'

He jerked out a chair and pointed. With a thankful sigh, she complied with his unspoken order. 'See what I mean?' he tossed over his shoulder, making for the shower upstairs.

All the same, she had the kettle boiling by the time he reappeared, heartbreakingly vital, glowing with health, clean-shirted and agile. His fitness made Jan overwhelmingly conscious of her still weakened state, and she longed to run into those toughly muscled arms and borrow some of their strength to see her through.

But it seemed those arms were not for her any more. Rik did not make the slightest move to touch her, nor even to look at her any more than normal, everyday conversation required.

Her dream-turned-nightmare that the parting of the ways had arrived seemed to have come dismayingly true. What had she done, she wondered, pretending to read the morning paper, to be put on to his private 'banned' list?

After the meal, she insisted on helping him to clear away the breakfast things.

Out of nowhere came the words, 'I want to talk to you, Janetta.'

Heart sinking to the very depths, she nodded and followed him into the living-room. Pushing his hands into his trouser pockets, he announced, faceless, expressionless, eyes empty, 'I'm releasing you from our marriage deal. From this moment on, you're free to go your own way. The verbal contract between us—and that's all there ever has been—has become null and void.'

CHAPTER ELEVEN

JAN thought she would faint. It wasn't true, she tried to tell herself, it was her mind starting to wander, still not completely recovered from her terrible ordeal.

That feeling she had lost about their lives diverting into different pathways—it had all been in her mind; not once had she given voice to the thought. Rik's constant attention during her recovery —it had surely demonstrated just how much she meant to him . . . Hadn't it?

'I see,' she said, trying to gather her wits and running her tongue over her dry lips. 'Which means I'm free?'

He nodded. 'Free of me entirely.'

It was imperative that she should sit down before her legs gave way. What was she supposed to say? 'I'm delighted to hear it', as if he had just given her some wonderful news?

'But——'

'The money?' he broke in. 'It's yours to keep. That at least I owe you.'

He came to sit on the arm of her chair, thighs tautly outlined, disturbingly close. 'You see,' he looked down into her wide, uncertain eyes, 'I've discovered your secret.'

'About my parents? You accept that they needed the money? You believe me now?' Jan exclaimed, her cheeks warm with relief.

'I believe you now. I know it wasn't your wish to

hide the truth about them. I know the whole story.'

'Did—did they tell you? As their prospective son-in-law?' Which he wasn't now, she had to remind herself.

'No, I heard it from Morris Wilkinson, my bank manager. A banking friend of his is a keen yachtsman and Steele & Mountford recently designed and built a boat for him. This friend knew Tom Fuller, your parents' bank manager. They met at a conference and Mr Fuller passed on the news about us. When I consulted Morris Wilkinson on business the other day, he congratulated me on my forthcoming marriage to the daughter of two of his friend Tom Fuller's customers—Edward and Penelope Hart. Unfortunate, he called them. He took it for granted that I knew their story and was surprised when I told him I didn't.'

'It was their pride,' Jan put in. 'They wouldn't let me tell you even when I asked permission.'

Rik nodded. 'Morris told me Tom Fuller had mentioned to him confidentially how their luck had seemed to take a turn for the better after my engagement to their daughter. He naturally, and rightly, assumed I had been behind their change of fortune, which in a sense was true, although it had happened without my knowledge. Having gone as far as he had, at my request and in the strictest confidence, he told me the rest, but only in view of my pending entry into the Hart family.'

'He told you why my father resigned from his job?' Jan asked eagerly. 'He hadn't done anything wrong, you understand that?'

'I understand everything now. Your father is one of the old school, he has rarity value,' Rik commented drily. 'He's an honourable man. I admire him greatly for his courage in following the path his conscience dictated.'

Jan nodded. 'I can't keep that money you gave me, Rik. It would be under false pretences if I did, wouldn't it? Splitting up, as we're going to do,' she wondered how she could speak the fateful words so calmly, 'I wouldn't be keeping my side of the bargain.'

'I told you,' he moved away from her, 'I've released you from that bargain.' He faced her. 'I can afford it. That money means nothing to me. In any case, if I demanded it back—money your parents have obviously already spent—it would be plunging them back into the chasm they've just struggled out of, financially speaking. Socially speaking too.'

'They're just beginning to hold up their heads again,' Jan agreed softly. 'Which is what has motivated me all through—the job offer from your father, the marriage deal with you.'

'I guessed.' Rik paused. 'They got themselves a fine, unselfish daughter when they had you. But there's no need any longer, Janetta, for you to present yourself to me as a sacrificial offering.'

He turned away, getting himself a drink, asking with his back to her, 'What's yours?'

'Nothing, thank you.'

He drank, staring through the window. 'I've offered your father a job within the merged company. He was delighted and told me he'd consider it.'

Which surely meant, Jan thought, her spirits lifting minutely, that, even when she and Rik had parted, there would at least be that link between them, tenuous though it might be.

'That was very good of you, Rik. Of course he'll take it. I'm sure it was just that darned pride of his making him pretend to hesitate.'

'I guessed that too.'

'And——' dared she ask? But with things the way they were between them, she probably wouldn't have another opportunity. 'Would you consider giving Tony——'

'His old job back? No.' Rik turned to view Jan's face, leaning against the fireplace, smiling at her dismay.

'But, Rik, his mother's going short of money——'

'Before you start abusing me, I've offered him a job. I was so impressed by what he'd done with *Riverjoy*—it even stood up well to the battering it got from the upset around the weir—I've taken him away from the admin side and put him into the boatbuilding section.'

'Rik, that's wonderful! Was he pleased?'

'Very. Like a two-tailed dog.'

'I'm so glad to hear it. Thank you for that.'

'You're very concerned about him. Is there something between you, after all?'

'Friendship, nothing else. How could there be?'

To her relief, he didn't ask her to explain that statement.

Did they have to be so stiff with each other, Jan thought, so distant after all that had passed between them? Her throat was filling, her eyes threatening to let the tears through. She had to escape before giving herself away.

Watching her go to the door, Rik said, 'There's no need for you to leave here yet. Take your time and find a place to your liking.'

'Thanks. I—I might just take you up on your offer.' She made it quickly to the top of the stairs, which was just as well, she thought, going into her

room as the tears might have blinded her, making her
miss her step.

He's telling me to go to get me out of his hair . . . to
leave the field clear so that he can carry on his affair
with Nadia. The words went round and round in
Jan's head as she lay on the bed, spent with crying.

Soon afterwards, Rik left the house. She was glad
that he hadn't disturbed her. She would have hated
him to have seen her tear-stained face. He would
have smiled pityingly, and left her for Nadia's arms.

When the telephone rang, she dived for it. Was he
ringing to say, 'Don't go, Janetta, I've discovered I
can't live without you'?

It was Rik, but all he said was, 'I'm at the
boatyard. You'll know where I am if you want me.'

'Why should I want you?' she answered thickly.
'I'm not your responsibility any more.' The receiver
crashing down from her hand ended the call.

Springing up, Jan seized her cases and piled her
belongings into them. She couldn't be there when he
came home. If they met again she would give herself
away, and that would be *her* pride ground into the
dust.

'You're free to go your own way,' Rik said,
dismissing her, his conscience clear because of the
money he had allowed her to keep. If only she were
free to leave that behind her too! She had paid dearly
for protecting her parents' pride . . .

About to close the front door, she hesitated. The
telephone was ringing. She would answer it once
more, but if it was Rik, she would hang up.

'Jan, my dear?' Raymond asked.

'Oh, Raymond, I——'

'What's this I hear about you and Richard

breaking up?'

'It's true, Raymond. He's discovered why I wanted the money——'

'I've just got the news from him and he told me the whole story.'

'So,' she went on bitterly, 'he's forgiven me for—for——' her lips quivered, 'for speaking the truth, and—dismissed me from the "job" he gave me. He d-doesn't want me as his wife any more.'

'Jan, my dear, are you crying? For God's sake, child, tell me why. You love him, you told me. Do you still feel the same?'

'I—I always will, Raymond, but that's my bad luck, isn't it?''

'Have you told him?'

'And have it thrown back in my face? You know how cynical he is about women in his life. "Wives are out", you said he told you, whereas women can come and go. I c-came, I'm going. I was just leaving when you rang. I've packed my cases and——'

'Jan, stay! That ring he gave you—ask him about it.'

'He told me—it was his mother's. He need worry, I'll leave it behind. I realise how precio must be to him.'

'Listen, Jan! Please—do one more thing before you go. *Ask him about that* promise?'

'All right, if that's what you want, I see him again. But it won't make Raymond. This is goodbye. To— been so nice knowing you——'

There was a strangled shout 'Jan, listen to me——'

The front door burst

Raymond . . .'

'Thank God for that. Ask him, do you hear, ask him!'

The receiver rattled into place as Jan's shaking hand released it.

'What do you want?' Jan spun round, putting as much fire into her voice as she could manage. 'I'm on my way out.'

Rik's fists hit his hips, his mood dangerous. 'To the Merry Maid's Arms, I suppose?'

'You suppose right. Anywhere, so long as it's away from you.' She crossed her fingers so that he wouldn't guess how her heart was breaking.

'So you're not my responsibility any more?'

She faced up to him. 'No, I'm not. It's my turn now. I quote your words. "I'm releasing you from our marriage deal. You're free to go your own way." 'o whatever you want, have whichever woman Especially if her name's Nadia.'

Jan dived for the door. Rik was the cases from her hands pelling her into the stay here until you do.'

'At least that'll keep you out of Nadia Beech's arms!' she spat.

'Jealous, are you?'

'That's the last thing I am,' she retaliated. But she was, and it tore at her insides. 'You've spent so much time with her lately, you might as well tell her husband to move over and join her permanently. You're throwing me out, just as you threw out all your father's other messengers, except you've delayed it a bit this time.'

'Let's deal with those points you've just made,' he answered, his manner now maddeningly businesslike. 'One, if I want any woman's arms, it's certainly not Nadia Beech's. If there's been any relationship between us at all, it was her intellect that drew me, not her physical charms. Her husband can keep her, with my blessing.'

'But——' Jan was bewildered, 'you've seen her almost every day!'

'Not completely accurate, but whenever I have met her, or contacted her by phone, it's been on a purely professional level, whatever other impression she might have tried to give. She's involved in the merger of Dancing River with Steele Construction. Before that, with Dancing River alone.'

This Jan had to accept, and she did so to the accompaniment of a pounding, hopeful heart.

'Two, I am not "throwing you out". I said you could stay as long as you wanted. Three, I treated my father's other messengers in the way they deserved. They were all—with one exception—on the make, gold-diggers to a woman.'

Jan moistened her lips, taking a step away from him, but he merely closed the gap, arms still folded.

'Who—who was the exception?'

'Coy, aren't we?'

'You mean me?' Her forefinger tapped her chest. 'But I accepted your money, didn't I, and your proposal of marriage?'

'Tell me why, Janetta.' There was a glint in Rik's eye and a note in his voice that made her pulses leap. All the same, she shook her head. Parting as they were he would never get the truth out of her.

But she had reckoned without his determination, his forcefulness when he wanted something. He seized her shoulders, dragging her against him.

'I'll get it out of you,' he vowed through his teeth, 'if I have to lock you up until you do. How would you like that, my beautiful messenger—being my prisoner, at my mercy?'

'Oh, Rik, I——'

His mouth coming down in a cruel, all-consuming kiss cut off her words and stole her breath completely away. Her hands clawed at his shoulders for support, even as she tried her utmost to tear her mouth from his.

Then, without warning, without even telling her brain what it was doing, her body began to yield, to submit to his demands, to give him kiss for ardent kiss. When he finally raised his head, her face was suffused with colour, her eyes the blue of the sky on a summer's day.

'Now will you tell me?' he ground out.

'Oh, Rik,' her head found his chest, her ear picked up the thud of his heart, 'I'll say it this once, then I'll go. I'll never trouble you again. I—I——'

'Well, come on,' he filled in impatiently.

'I—I love you. There,' Jan tried to prise herself away from his hold, 'now you can laugh and say you pity me, because, too bad for me, a wife's a non-starter where your lifestyle's concerned. And,' she threw her head, 'I'll never live with you as your woman. You see, I know that, deep down, you wouldn't respect me. I'll never dance to your tune, because I know exactly what your tune is. I'd be just another female passing through your life. So let me go, Rik, and I'll——'

'Let you go?' His eyes were so bright now, she thought she could see twin suns shining out. 'O-oh no, lady, not now, not ever.'

He pulled her down to the sofa, pushing her back. Her hair spread out against the cushions, her lips parting as her breath came quickly. Rik looked deep into her eyes, a hand wrapping round her throat, the other playing with a strand of her hair.

'I understand,' he said, the lines of his face taut and determined, 'that my father gave you a message too . . . something you wanted to ask me?'

'About this ring.' She held it up. 'But I know the answer. It's very precious to you because it was your mother's.'

'That's part of the answer. Shall I tell you the other?'

Jan nodded, holding her breath.

'A long time ago I told my father that the woman I eventually gave that ring to would be the woman I'd love to the end of my days. She would be the one I intended to marry. The moment I saw you, I knew beyond doubt that you were the one.'

Jan, eyes shining, asked wonderingly, 'From the day we met, you've loved me?'

'Why so astonished? Weren't my actions in these past few days enough to tell you——'

'All they told me was that you could hardly

stand me around and that you couldn't wait to give me my marching orders and get the house to yourself again!'

'You can't mean it?' Could his eyebrows go any higher? Jan wondered bemusedly, tracing them with her finger and wondering also if she was in the middle of a beautiful dream and would wake up soon to stark reality . . .

'You were so distant, darling,' she sighed, 'and so cold, I nearly died.'

'By then I knew the truth about your parents, and why you needed that money so desperately. Which meant that I couldn't hold you to your promise any longer. It also meant the end of our relationship. So for my own sake I didn't dare lay anything but an impersonal hand on you. And I couldn't forget that note you left. You told me I'd poisoned your feelings——'

'Only because I couldn't think of any way of making you believe me when I told you the truth about myself.'

'By the time I got that note, I believed you all right, but you'd gone. But I have to say it, my love, when I eventually got you safely back on dry land, you were so stiff and starchy with me, and without the very valid reason which I had for holding off, it twisted me up inside to see the dislike in your eyes.'

'*Dis*like?' Jan exploded, trying to wriggle free in her indignation. 'If you knew how much I longed for you to take me in your arms——'

'Like this?' Rik stood, pulling her on to his lap, his hand sliding under her top and caressing her breasts until her arms wound around his neck. Then his mouth came down and he kissed her until she responded with a wild abandon.

He buried his face in her neck. 'The sweetness of you,' he said huskily, 'the beauty of your body, the loveliness of your face . . . All through these past three or four days, when I've seen you and touched you, yet had to rein in my overwhelming desire to grab you and make passionate, endless love to you, it's been like living in hell and glimpsing a heaven beyond my reach.'

'Yet you as good as told me to go. For heaven's sake, why, darling?'

'I had to. I felt it was my duty. I'd persuaded you, as I thought, against your will to agree to marry me. Then I discovered your reason for agreeing—which wasn't through love of me, was it?' Rik pressed her nose.

'Oh, yes, it was! I was crazy about you from the moment I saw you. In fact,' Jan shifted and he moved too, and she curled into a more comfortable position on his lap, 'I have to confess, darling, even *before* I met you. Your father had given me that photo of you to help me identify you. By the time I'd arrived at your house and, with Tony's unintentional help, gatecrashed your party, I knew every one of your features by heart.'

'Oh, did you? And——'

The telephone rang and, with a mild expletive, Rik reached out for it, maintaining his hold on her body, caressing her as he talked.

'Father? Yes, we're fine, all is forgiven. She's going to marry me.' He turned to her and his raised eyebrows prompted a response. She nodded emphatically, mouthing the words, 'Yes, please, darling,' and he laughed.

'We're fixing the wedding date, and,' he went on, with a simmering glance at the girl he was holding, 'it had better be soon. Otherwise she might take it into her lovely head to go for another unexpected dip in the River Thames, and I'm going to make sure that from now on I'll be beside her, to haul her out before she even hits the water!' He listened with a smile and glanced again at Jan, who was gazing up at him with near-adoration.

'OK, I'll tell her. Great to hear it, Father. Now, will you allow us to get on with——' There was laughter from the other end, the call being hastily disconnected.

'My father says,' Rik turned back to Jan, 'that he and Celia are getting on so well together, they're seriously considering making their friendship into a permanent partnership.'

'That's wonderful, Rik!'

'He also says he's delighted he decided to take over from you the role of go-between, so that he could bring the most stupid couple he knows—in fact, the couple he loves most in the world— together again.'

'Mission accomplished,' she sighed, smiling into his brilliant eyes. 'This messenger's signing off. I'll dance to your tune for the rest of my life.'

'And I, my beloved, to yours.'

Jan smiled with shy provocation.

'You can come into this "merry maid's arms" any time you like,' she said, holding them out.

'Right,' Rik replied, lifting her with an anticipatory gleam in his eyes, and striding with her up the stairs, 'prepare yourself, my merry maid, because I'm about to take you at your word . . .'

HARLEQUIN'S "BIG WIN"
SWEEPSTAKES RULES & REGULATIONS
NO PURCHASE NECESSARY TO ENTER OR RECEIVE A PRIZE

1. To enter and join the Reader Service, scratch off the metallic strips on all your BIG WIN tickets #1-#6. This will reveal the values for each sweepstakes entry number, the number of free book(s) you will receive, and your free bonus gift as part of our Reader Service. If you do not wish to take advantage of our Reader Service, but wish to enter the Sweepstakes only, scratch off the metallic strips on your BIG WIN tickets #1-#4. Return your entire sheet of tickets intact. Incomplete and/or inaccurate entries are ineligible for that section or sections of prizes. Not responsible for mutilated or unreadable entries or inadvertent printing errors. Mechanically reproduced entries are null and void.

2. Whether you take advantage of this offer or not, your Sweepstakes numbers will be compared against a list of winning numbers generated at random by the computer. In the event that all prizes are not claimed by March 31, 1992, a random drawing will be held from all qualified entries received from March 30, 1990 to March 31, 1992, to award all unclaimed prizes. All cash prizes (Grand to Sixth), will be mailed to the winners and are payable by cheque in U.S. funds. Seventh prize is to be shipped to winners via third-class mail. These prizes are in addition to any free, surprise or mystery gifts that might be offered. Versions of this sweepstakes with different prizes of approximate equal value may appear in other mailings or at retail outlets by Torstar Corp. and its affiliates.

3. The following prizes are awarded in this sweepstakes: ★ Grand Prize (1) $1,000,000; First Prize (1) $25,000; Second Prize (1) $10,000; Third Prize (5) $5,000; Fourth Prize (10) $1,000; Fifth Prize (100) $250; Sixth Prize (2500) $10; ★ ★ Seventh Prize (6000) $12.95 ARV.

   ★ This Sweepstakes contains a Grand Prize offering of $1,000,000 annuity. Winner will receive $33,333.33 a year for 30 years without interest totalling $1,000,000.

   ★ ★ Seventh Prize: A fully illustrated hardcover book published by Torstar Corp. Approximate value of the book is $12.95.

   Entrants may cancel the Reader Service at any time without cost or obligation to buy (see details in center insert card).

4. This promotion is being conducted under the supervision of Marden-Kane, Inc., an independent judging organization. By entering this Sweepstakes, each entrant accepts and agrees to be bound by these rules and the decisions of the judges, which shall be final and binding. Odds of winning in the random drawing are dependent upon the total number of entries received. Taxes, if any, are the sole responsibility of the winners. Prizes are nontransferable. All entries must be received by no later than 12:00 NOON, on March 31, 1992. The drawing for all unclaimed sweepstakes prizes will take place May 30, 1992, at 12:00 NOON, at the offices of Marden-Kane, Inc., Lake Success, New York.

5. This offer is open to residents of the U.S., the United Kingdom, France and Canada, 18 years or older except employees and their immediate family members of Torstar Corp., its affiliates, subsidiaries, Marden-Kane, Inc., and all other agencies and persons connected with conducting this Sweepstakes. All Federal, State and local laws apply. Void wherever prohibited or restricted by law. Any litigation respecting the conduct and awarding of a prize in this publicity contest may be submitted to the Régie des loteries et courses du Québec.

6. Winners will be notified by mail and may be required to execute an affidavit of eligibility and release which must be returned within 14 days after notification or, an alternative winner will be selected. Canadian winners will be required to correctly answer an arithmetical skill-testing question administered by mail which must be returned within a limited time. Winners consent to the use of their names, photographs and/or likenesses for advertising and publicity in conjunction with this and similar promotions without additional compensation.

7. For a list of our major winners, send a stamped, self-addressed envelope to: WINNERS LIST c/o MARDEN-KANE, INC., P.O. BOX 701, SAYREVILLE, NJ 08871. Winners Lists will be fulfilled after the May 30, 1992 drawing date.

If Sweepstakes entry form is missing, please print your name and address on a 3" ×5" piece of plain paper and send to:

In the U.S.
Harlequin's "BIG WIN" Sweepstakes
901 Fuhrmann Blvd.
P.O. Box 1867
Buffalo, NY 14269-1867

In Canada
Harlequin's "BIG WIN" Sweepstakes
P.O. Box 609
Fort Erie, Ontario
L2A 5X3

© 1989 Harlequin Enterprises Limited   Printed in the U.S.A.

LTY-H590

Have You Ever Wondered If You Could Write A Harlequin Novel?

Here's great news—Harlequin is offering a series of cassette tapes to help you do just that. Written by Harlequin editors, these tapes give practical advice on how to make your characters—and your story—come alive. There's a tape for each contemporary romance series Harlequin publishes.

Mail order only

All sales final
